FOR LOVE OF ZACHARY

By

Kathleen V. McLennan

© 2019

TABLE OF CONTENTS

Zachary was born into such a cocoon of love. He should have grown in grace and beauty, and when he didn't, they all blamed Zachary. But it wasn't his fault entirely; the threads had started unraveling long before he came on the scene. He would never know the truth of his own story unless fate dealt a trick card in the game of life. And what did it have to do with a loner like Bruno?

Bruno, on a community order, has his own problems to deal with. He just has to clock up his community order and put up with the two old ladies until his hours are up. After that, well, nothing is ever really going to change for him, is it?

CHAPTER ONE

The old lady was already out on her little verandah peering over the lone rosebush when Bruno walked up the narrow roadway between the delightful retirement villas of the oldies' village.

"Oh, geez! Trust me to get the stickybeak!"

Bruno's 'stickybeak' was a resident in the sprawling retirement estate, not far from the community-run share house where he boarded.

After a spate of media reports about bag snatchers, louts, harassment of pensioners, and frail old people being attacked in their homes, the local churches had looked with alarm at their aging - and diminishing worshippers. Then they had joined forces with the various Government departments to build the Seven Plains Retirement Village.

The whole district had underestimated the feelings of insecurity of its aging population. Half the units were pre-sold before they were finished, and already the village had been extended beyond its original size. Church services were moved to a new chapel at Seven Plains, and the red brick Sunday schools were re-furbished as youth services or drop-in centers for single parents.

Aware of their other community roles, the churches had also organized what they called their Community Inclusion Project. This project was a co-operative venture with the Department of Corrections, encouraging community service orders for early offenders rather than prison sentences. The reasoning was that if the transgressing youngsters knew the old people, they'd be less likely to prey on them.

Bruno was typical of their case studies. From his boyhood, he had chosen the role of class clown to cover his lack of skills in the classroom, thriving only when he was outside or on the sporting field. Unfortunately, his bursts of aggression forced him off the field far too often to learn about sportsmanship. He skipped classes during his early secondary schooling and left well before being legally able to do so. He had no job in mind and very little likelihood that he would ever be able to keep one, should any opportunity present itself. A railway guard had locked him in the guard's van, then put him off the train for traveling without a ticket, 'to make an example of him'. Following this, a supermarket security guard had him charged with shoplifting some ready-to-eat food because he hadn't eaten for 18 hours.

This wasn't Bruno's first community service order. Still, he hated the curiosity that always stirred up stuff he'd rather not remember. He knew the oldies had been warned not to pry too much. They would ask for a name, and Bruno could elect to use a different name, as long as he kept it for the duration. But they need give no surnames or answer questions about their offenses, charges, or case histories. Just give a name, tick the box, do the job, get the community hours up, and that's it!

"Hello." Her voice wasn't as crinkly sounding as he'd thought it would be. He gave a short glance upwards at her and then dropped his head, discouraging too much talk. All these oldies looked the same to him – wrinkled, flimsy, and used up. "Are you assigned to me?"

"Yeah… yes," he corrected. He needed a good report this time if he didn't want to find himself on the wrong side of a very high wall.

"Oh good! I'm Mrs. Dwyer," she said and waited for a response. Bruno remained silent. There was an over-long pause. "What would you like me to call you?"

The careful wording pinged in Bruno's mind. The old bat knew the ropes already. She must have had contact with the justice system before. That meant he'd need to be extra careful. Quickly discarding some of his nicknames, such as Bruiser and Brute, he muttered, "Bruno."

"Good name!" She cocked her head, rather like a magpie inspecting a potential meal. "Strong! Resilient, like a bear." She gave a short chuckle. Then, before he could get annoyed, she became very business-like. "Your supervisor isn't with you. Has he told you what needs to be done?"

"Yes. He's sorting out the new kids. They said the bluestone pitchers in the back garden all have to be taken out."

"That's right. I'm afraid there are quite a lot of them, and because the roadway here is so narrow, they have to be stacked on the traffic island down past number 21." She pointed to the house at the end, where the roads intersected. The estate was ready for a new extension of the village beyond the existing cyclone wire fence. It was the only vacant space Bruno had seen since he'd signed in at the office.

"I can handle 'em," he said. "Someone's bringing around a wheelbarrow later."

"Just wait there a moment," Mrs. Dwyer called as she disappeared inside. The garage door rumbled and rose to show not a garage, but a carport, with access to the back yard. From the look of the floor, no car had ever dropped a spot of grease on the pristine concrete. Except for a few gardening tools, a mop, and a bucket, the carport contained only a folded wheelchair. "You can come in and out through here without having to bother me at all!" she said reassuringly.

"Hmm!" Bruno nodded. *"What about her not bothering him?"* he wondered. He stepped through to the backyard and gave an involuntary gasp. "GEEZ!"

The backyard was small, even smaller than the flat that was his last remembered home. The garden had been built up with bluestone pitchers and the plants had gone berserk through sheer lack of pruning and maintenance. Clinging festoons of white jasmine tumbled over purple happy wanderer and thornless yellow roses; their flowers twisted into each other in riotous abundance. Tall stems of spent gladioli leaned over each other; their individual blooms shouldered aside by small flowering shrubs that leaned over the edge of the bluestones, roots grasping wherever they could. Shriveled yellow-brown leaves of long-departed daffodils wilted on the daisies beneath. Ground cover spread over the surface and down the stone wall in long, leggy strands. There was scarcely room to move in what little space was left along the path.

"My late husband was in a wheelchair," Mrs. Dwyer explained. "He couldn't bend to garden. He did so love his plants."

"He sure must have!" Bruno could not have stopped the comment. He couldn't tell where one plant ended and the other started. "Do they all have to come out first?"

Mrs. Dwyer nodded.

"Mmm. I'm afraid the pruning is beyond me now." She held up a clawed hand, and Bruno saw how little movement she had left in her wrist. He flexed his own strong brown hands to insure them against such a curse. "I have some hessian bags for them to go into, and the maintenance man will help me decide which ones to keep when the ground is leveled again. I just hate parting with any of them. They're like children to me."

Bruno was tempted to say, "Well, that should make 'em easier to get rid of!" But wisely kept his mouth shut. *"Children,"* he thought. He knew about getting rid of children. *"Easy. Just take 'im to the children's home and tell them he's uncontrollable."* Just take 'im to the children's home and tell them' he's uncontrollable." Unwilling to see it again, but certain that his memory was absolutely accurate, he still felt that hole in his gut when his mother shut the green door behind her and left him in that reception hall; the two short bench seats, the vague smell of disinfectant, and the endless grey corridors that defined his new state of existence. He was 12 and homeless, a ward of the state. He shook the memory away. "Plenty of colors to choose from," he said, sounding almost friendly, in a sudden wish not to be so inside his own mind. "Some of 'em are real pretty!"

Mrs. Dwyer beamed. "Oh, it's so nice to have someone who appreciates them! It's the snapdragons, of course. They bring such lightness into such a small place, don't you think?"

Bruno didn't think, mainly because he didn't know which ones were the snapdragons. There were some tall plants with colorful tops, so he took a chance and pointed to them without actually naming them. "Those yellow ones are pretty bright."

"Yes, they're the ones! And those pink ones over there, alongside the dark crimson ones. This is their third year!" She sounded so impressed; Bruno risked being impressed too.

"Third year? They've lasted well!"

"Haven't they? Normally they're biennials, you know."

Bruno fell silent. What was a biennial for the love of Mike?

"But Desmond wouldn't pull them out, you see. He used to say, 'Well, we got our two years' worth. Let's see if we get a bonus year!' And he left them in."

"*Okay,*" Bruno thought, "*Biennial must mean plants that last two years. Did that mean a one-ennial was a one-year plant, and a triathlon - no - triennial would last three years?*" "Will I bag snapdragons up first?"

"No, leave them until last, because they'll just go in the rubbish. They can't last another year, but we might as well enjoy them for as long as we can." Bruno felt a sudden surge of heat at the casual dismissal of the stupid plants. They were doing what they were supposed to do, better even, and they were just going to get chucked away in the rubbish. It wasn't fair! It must have shown on his face because Mrs. Dwyer said quietly, "I have some empty pots. You could pot them up and take them home with you if you like."

Bruno shrugged off his anger, masking his emotion. "Nah," he said, "I'll just leave 'em until I've done all the others. Where do I put the plants?"

"Oh, you can stack the hessian bags around the rosebush out the front. But you'll have to cut a lot off them before we can bag them up." She reached for a table beside her and handed Bruno a pair of secateurs. "All the clippings will go in the green waste."

She pointed to the bin just alongside the carport. "You can roll it out the front before you leave tonight."

"Okay, missus."

"Mrs. Dwyer," she corrected.

Bruno scowled. "Okay, Mrs. Dwyer."

He took the secateurs, ignored the standard-issue cotton gloves in his pocket and grabbed a handful of happy wanderers. His hard yank gave voice to a satisfying crunch as he dragged the vine off the rear wall. Some of the jasmine came down with it.

"This is going to be a done deal," he thought, clasping the fragile-looking jasmine. He yanked sharply, and the string-thin vines slashed across the palm of his hand. "Ouch! Shit!" he yelped as the thin strands sliced like wire into his flesh.

Mrs. Dwyer looked concerned. "That jasmine is the very devil of a vine to pull out. Are you bleeding?"

Bruno inspected the slash. "Yeah," he said, "a bit... quite a bit."

"Let's have a look." Mrs. Dwyer reached towards his hand. Instinctively Bruno pulled back in a movement that was sheer self-defense. "I'm not going to amputate it," the old lady said mildly. "I just wanted to see if it needs a stitch or a band-aid."

"Band-aid'll do," Bruno said gruffly. He wished he hadn't reacted like that, but years of learning to dodge sudden blows made the movement automatic.

"Had a tetanus shot?" The question niggled at his brain for a moment.

"When I was a kid," he said doubtfully. "I fell into a drainage vent down the creek."

"Hm. You might need a booster by now. Should I ring your supervisor?"

Bruno looked alarmed. He didn't want any reports going in about carelessness or injury. "It's not that bad, really. I'll wash it."

Mrs. Dwyer read his alarm pretty accurately. "Come inside, and we'll get some disinfectant on it and a proper bandage. Then you can tell your supervisor later if it starts to get hot or shows any redness."

"Well, all right," he muttered as he followed her into the unit. It was small and not all that tidy, but everything seemed comfortable where it was. The bathroom was tiny, like a motel en-suite. Bruno remembered a few they'd stayed at when he was little. His mum would lay him on the divan, his face to the wall, and wrap the spare blankets around him. He turned away from the memory before the noises started pounding inside his head.

"Everything you need is in the first aid box. If you can't manage the band-aid, bring it out with you, and I'll fix it on when you're ready." With that, Mrs. Dwyer left him to it. Still, Bruno locked the little latch - just in case she was a weirdo. The vine had sliced quite deeply into his hand, and the leaves, turning back on their tough little knobs, had gouged the wound deeper as he'd dragged them. Bruno had plenty of experience with disinfectants and band-aids. When he emerged, Mrs. Dwyer could see he needed no help from her. "Well, I don't think a doctor could have done it any better!" she said in some surprise. Bruno felt a small surge of satisfaction. There! That'd show the old duck he wasn't stupid or anything! "I made some tea with plenty of sugar. Do you take milk?"

"I drink coffee," he said.

"Medicinal," she answered laconically, "in case there's delayed shock."

"Oh. Then milk... please." God, it was an effort to remember the stupid manners the supervisor had parroted at them. Please and thank you. Use the proper titles, Mr. or Mrs. or Ms., not Jean or Gary, unless they specifically ask you to use first names.

Mrs. Dwyer handed him the sweet, milky tea. It surprised him that the warmth seemed to reach his hand and ease the stinging.

"Er, thanks," he mumbled.

"There's a biscuit if you want one."

Mrs. Dwyer placed a saucer with half a dozen biscuits on it. He ate four before he even thought about it. She eyed him thoughtfully. "Had breakfast early, did you?"

"Six-thirty." He didn't say that if you waited until seven, there was hardly anything left. She seemed to know that anyway because she put out another six biscuits. "I'm not supposed to eat them these days, so you may as well finish them off."

Bruno did so. When he finished his drink, he turned to leave.

"I think you'd better use these." The old lady was holding out some heavy leather gardening gloves. "They'll protect your hands from more damage."

"Thanks. I won't be yanking that stuff down like that again."

"Good to know you're a fast learner!" she said mildly.

Bruno blinked at that. All his life he had been called a lot of things; dumb, dopey, retard, even dyslexic. Never in his life had he been called a fast learner. He knew he wasn't dyslexic because he could read pretty well now. His math wasn't too bad either for money and stuff, as long as he had a bit of time. The children's home had done that at least. The teachers there seemed to understand how things were. They even had a punching bag in the little room that served as a cloakroom. If you felt like busting someone's head, you could slip outside and spend a couple of minutes on the punching bag instead. Lots of the kids used it, not just him. He didn't feel like such a dickhead there. The kids at his old school used to sneer at him when it came to general knowledge. He'd never been anywhere, never owned a picture book, and never been told anything much about the world beyond what he saw in his own street or on TV. What did he know about circuses and holidays at the beach or Grandpa's farm? He supposed he must have had a grandpa or two once, but he'd never met any of 'em! So now he was a fast learner? "Yeah - well, pain is a quick teacher." He went out and began work again, this time with the gloves and secateurs.

For the next two hours, Bruno worked steadily along the vines, cutting back the longest strands and using the curved end of a small hoe to drag them free as far as he could. Then he attacked the lower ends with the secateurs. The green bin was full to overflowing with trailing vines when he walked it out the front to its allotted place. It seemed to him that the oldies should also have an allotted place where they could be wheeled to as they died off. *"I wonder what they do with the dead bodies when they cark it?"* he mused. *"They can't last long, and there is a lot of 'em."* He saw the supervisor approaching and straightened up as though he were putting in a big effort - which in truth, he had.

"Hi, Bruno. How's it going?"

"Fair enough." Bruno shrugged.

He had no beef with this supervisor. He wasn't narking at them all the time, and he had trusted Bruno enough to let him start unaccompanied this morning. Bruno could have lagged off, but he knew it would come back to bite him if he did. They'd just add more hours on the other end or even give him a community sentence at a detention center, and he didn't want that. He'd heard enough to steer clear if he could. He'd already learned from his mates they could be pretty brutal places, especially if you were on the small side. Bruno wasn't above thumping someone if he had to, but he hated to see the big bullies picking on weaklings and little squirts. To him, that just wasn't fair. This supervisor seemed fair.

"There's a sandwich bar in the reception area. We're getting some lunch there and eating out in the front garden. Plenty of tables there. You ready for a break?"

"Yeah, I'll just tell Missus…"

"Mrs… Dwyer," came the interruption as she emerged onto her tiny porch and nodded at the supervisor.

"Dwyer," amended Bruno, peeling off the heavy gloves and handing them to her.

The supervisor frowned. "Where are the gloves you were issued with?"

Before Bruno could haul them out of his pocket, Mrs. Dwyer spoke again, to the supervisor this time.

"Those cotton gloves were not suitable at all for pulling down vines. They tear too easily. Look at this!" She waved a cotton glove at the supervisor. It was torn across the palm in much the same way as his hand.

The supervisor shot a glance at Bruno's hand and saw the bandage. "Is it a bad injury?" he asked. "You might need a tetanus shot."

Bruno shook his head. He knew he would have got a serve for not wearing his gloves straight off, but where the hell had Mrs. Dwyer got her torn glove from? Well, there was no way he was going to pull out the untouched gloves in his pocket.

He looked at her, puzzled. Then he started. Was he wrong, or did the old doddy just wink at him?

The supervisor looked at the bandage without actually inspecting it. "It's well-protected at any rate." He turned to Mrs. Dwyer, preparing to thank her.

"Did you dress it? It looks quite professional."

Mrs. Dwyer laughed. "Not me. I'm no nurse! No, Bruno did it himself."

The supervisor's eyes opened in surprise. "Well done! I don't think a nurse could have done better!" Bruno realized he had not only escaped a telling-off; he had also been complimented on his first-aid technique. For the first time that day, he grinned.

"I'll be back after lunch!" he said, sauntering after the supervisor, who turned back and said,

"No, you won't. We'll have a doctor check that hand and see about a tetanus shot. You'll be back tomorrow."

"Tomorrow then!" Bruno yelled over his shoulder.

CHAPTER TWO

Mrs. Dwyer watched them as far as the corner, then went back inside. She made fresh tea and cut herself a cheese sandwich. *"Why is it that these kids are all so sullen?"* she wondered. *"Here they are ready for their first taste of the world, and they already look like such sour-pusses!!"* She sipped her tea as she considered her new garden assistant. *"He arrived this morning looking like he'd push me over just for the fun of it."* Her eyes were thoughtful. *"But when he grinned like that, his face lit up like a Christmas tree! He must have been a beautiful little boy when he was young! I wonder what went wrong for him?"*

Mrs. Dwyer was no romantic. She knew perfectly well that being a beautiful child was no guarantee of success in life. But she also knew that if children were good-looking, they usually got more encouragement than kids who were less pleasant to look at. Her own younger brother had been born with a cleft palate, which left his top lip split open like a burst seedpod. Until he had his operation, he had suffered cruelly from the ignorant comments of children and grown-ups alike, who spoke of his misfortune in his presence as if he were deaf as well.

"Oh, my dear!" they would mouth their sympathy at her mother while almost preening that their own children were 'normal'.

"Will you be able to put him into a special school, or will you have to look after him at home?"

His mother would seethe but was too polite to give the acid response that was teetering upon her lips.

"He's actually quite bright and will go to the same school as the others."

"Oh, but surely they won't be able to admit him?" They had no idea how callous they were!

In the end Lawrie had proved himself. His operation - one of the first of its kind- had left only thin scars that gradually faded, and he became an accountant with the Star - Bowkett Building Society. "*Oh yes,*" thought Mrs. Dwyer, "*good looks can save you a lot of anguish.*"

She considered Bruno again. Obviously, his good looks hadn't been protection enough. Probably Italian, with a name like that - if it was his real name. Mid-teens - maybe 18? He was a big muscular fellow, with a face that knew the rough side of life, but he could have been younger. Say 17 then. He couldn't have done anything aggravated or with weapons, or they'd hardly have him working with secateurs. The thought crossed her mind that she had given him the secateurs, not them, whoever 'they' were. "I don't think I was putting my life at risk," she told herself aloud. But maybe that was just to reassure herself, because a sudden knock at the door made her jump.

"It's Gwen!" called her next-door neighbor. "How did it go?" Mrs. Dwyer got up, slightly jangled, and opened the door. Breathless with thwarted curiosity, Gwen hurried in, grabbing a cup and the teapot in one practiced move. She sat down and immediately poured herself a black tea. "Now," she said eagerly, "tell me how it all went!"

"Oh, quite well, actually. The young fellow they gave me has already put a bin-load of vines out, and that's about one-third of the jungle!"

"So, he's a worker. Good! Peg Thompson over at Olive Street said hers was a scrawny little fellow who spent most of the morning crying. He's picking weeds out of her gravel paths, and his knuckles were red raw by the time he went for lunch."

"Probably never done it before in his life."

Gwen felt sorry for the scrawny one already.

"You're right there. He lived on the twelfth floor of one of those high-rise rabbit warrens. He'd hardly ever see a real live garden on suicide hill."

"Suicide Hill?" Mrs. Dwyer frowned.

"That's what he called it," said Gwen, looking suitably upset. "20 stories high, and at least one death every couple of months. They jump!"

"Oh God!" whispered Mrs. Dwyer. "And the children see them?"

"Apparently." Gwen was nodding. "He told Mrs. Thompson that at least no-one would land on her driveway and splatter it, like the back parking lot where he lived."

"Ugh!" Mrs. Dwyer was horrified. "No child should have to see such things!"

"Maybe not. But there are more than 1,000 people over there, and probably 60 percent of them are children." Gwen nodded knowingly.

"Single mothers, desperate for housing they can afford." Mrs. Dwyer shook her head.

"It shouldn't have to be that way!"

Gwen nodded again and the two shared their tea break in silence, each a little relieved that such misfortune had never befallen them.

The doctor's surgery had a few afternoon patients lined up; when Bruno came in with the supervisor, they took him straight to the dressings room. The doctor checked the wound and pronounced it clean of infection. Then he left the nurse to re-dress it, and after that, they had a special form to complete. They all agreed Bruno could go back to work the next day. "Just as long as you wear good protective gloves and don't let any dirt get into the wound itself." The doctor noted that Bruno had been in after a skateboard incident a year or two earlier and had a tetanus booster then. "You won't need another. They're good for six or seven years."

A replacement supervisor would take care of the other kids, whilst this one, Steve, drove Bruno back to the community house. At first, there was silence between them. Then the supervisor said quietly, "It's good to know you were really doing the job in there. There's nothing fake about that wound."

"Fake? No. It's bloody sore!"

"Do you think you'll be up for it tomorrow? We could postpone for a day or two."

Bruno shook his head. "Nah! Hours are hours, and the more I clock up, the less I'll have to keep comin' back."

"Mm." The supervisor gave a sideward glance at the youth.

Normally Bruno didn't respond much to conversation. "And these hours are already add-ons?"

Bruno shrugged. "I took a day off," he said with a touch of defiance, "and went to the show."

"How did you get in?"

Bruno gave a small grin. "Easy! I picked up a bin that was overflowing and said to the bloke on the gate, 'Say boss, where do I empty this?' He pointed to an area inside the gate, and I just carried it through."

Steve laughed in spite of himself. "Well, if it was that easy, I can't say I'd blame you altogether!"

"Anyway, it was worth it. I'd never been to the show before." Maybe there was a trace of wistfulness in the comment, but Steve let it rest.

Bruno felt a bit more comfortable now, so he asked the question that had struck him earlier. "All those oldies, where do they put 'em when they die?"

The supervisor took another sideways look. "Well, now, that's a question!" he remarked.

"They call the doctor or an ambulance and they're taken to hospital. Then they notify their families to make the arrangements for their funeral."

Bruno frowned. "If they got families, why are they all here by themselves?"

"Well, some of them don't have any families, but most of them have somebody. It's just they are too old to manage by themselves anymore, or maybe they've had an injury, or arthritis, or something like that."

Bruno gave a slight shake of his head. "Mrs. Dwyer's got arthritis. Her hands are all screwed up like a claw. So, their families put 'em in the home?"

Steve paused before answering. "A lot of people sign themselves in because they don't feel they can manage anymore, and they don't want to be a burden to their families."

Bruno grunted. "Yeah, or the families don't want them to be a burden either."

Steve sensed the cynicism and tried again. "Sometimes with the best will in the world, a family just can't do the job. Some of these people need help with showers and feeding themselves. The ones in high care need nurses, not families. That's 24-hour care."

Bruno could see the difference. "But Mrs. Dwyer's not like that."

"No, but her husband was. When he had to come here, she came with him. They wanted to be together until he died."

Bruno considered this. "So, she put herself into the home?"

"That's it. Most of the old people want to be here. The world out there is tough, and it scares them. They feel safe and cared for here."

Bruno nodded. "I thought they might have to - you know - cremate them all on-site or something."

Steve looked at him but could think of nothing more to say, so they finished the ride in silence.

Except for the manager, the community house was almost empty. There were a couple of little kids clinging to their mother while she was re-directed to a women's safe house. Bruno didn't need to hear their story. He knew it intimately. The mum's bruised forehead, and the red finger marks still glowing on the older boy, a seven-year-old, told him their story plain and clear.

Which one had it been? Rick? No, he was the gambler. Rod - that was the one. As soon as there was any sign of a disagreement, his fuse would blow out, and wham! Mum would be flying back against the fridge, or the hot stove, or the wall if she were lucky. Bruno would fling himself at Rod, and he'd get an open hand across the face every time. Once, he got the closed fist and two of his teeth went flying. Luckily, they were his first teeth. By the time his second teeth had grown, Bruno had learned to duck.

Abruptly, he turned away. It was always the same when he started something new. While he was trying to make sense of it all, the memories would come up out of nowhere, haunting him and adding to his misery. He reached into the communal fridge and grabbed the iced coffee from his shelf. They didn't exactly forbid you to go to your room during the day. Still, it was the house policy to relax in the loungeroom so that the boarders (he nearly thought inmates) could get to know each other and maybe offer some kind of friendship. Bruno usually scorned the idea. Today, with his hand hurting and his mind full of sharp, painful memories, even daytime TV would be better than nothing. He sat down and began flicking through the channels.

"There's an old movie starting in a couple of minutes," said a froggy voice on his left. He turned to see a youth a bit smaller than himself, lying on the other couch with a blanket around him.

"Black and white or colored?" he asked casually.

"Black and white, I think. The manager said it was a good adventure story."

"Hmm. Better than 'The Bold and the Beautiful' anyway!" He settled back as the titles came up for 'Captains Courageous'.

At the start, both boys agreed it was old-fashioned and that the boy was a little smart-arse. As the story went on, they were pulled into the sheer adventure of his enforced life on a fishing trawler. The harshness, the brutality of the life, and the unlikely kinship that grew between the boy and his Portuguese mentor gave them something to think about. They watched in silence, and when the movie ended, Bruno turned the TV off rather than break the spell.

Eventually, the younger boy said, "He got a fishhook in his hand. What happened to yours?"

Bruno came back to the real world. "Oh, I was pulling out jasmine vines in a garden, and they cut into my skin. I had to get a tetanus shot," he lied to bolster the story. "What about you?"

"Food poisoning, they think. I ate some fish yesterday that smelt a bit off. I chucked most of it already."

"You should be okay by tomorrow. Food poisoning doesn't last long."

"How do you know?"

"One of our landladies used to tell us that every time we complained about her cooking."

"No shit! She could h've killed you!"

"That's why we left," said Bruno.

He didn't think it necessary to say they were two months behind with the rent. In those days, his mum used to say he was her lucky charm. He believed it too. He'd heard them calling out, "If it wasn't for that poor little soul, you'd have been out on your ear long before now! Buy him some food before you drink it all, you selfish cow!"

And his mother would stay sober just long enough to find some broken down single fronted terrace with a dilapidated room out the back and not too many questions at the front door. Then gradually, she would slide away down the neck of a bottle, and they'd be out on the streets again. Bruno shook the memories away. "I don't remember you here before. I'm Bruno."

"They call me Tanner."

"That your last name?"

"Nup. I think it's because I used to leg for a bookie, and I'd have to yell '10 to one on the outsider'. The boy gave a soft demonstration, "Tannerone on y' ousidah!"

"What's that mean?" asked Bruno, surprising himself. Normally he would never ask a question that might show him to be ignorant.

"It's racecourse lingo. It means the bookie will pay you 10 times the starting price if the outsider wins. People love betting on a long shot."

"But if he's an outsider, he's most likely to win, isn't he?" Tanner grinned.

"Nah. That's where the bookies make their money. They don't want everybody backing the favorite. They'd have to pay out too much!"

"My mum used to say betting was a mug's game," Bruno mumbled.

"She's right," said Tanner. "If you're a punter. Yer never see a rich punter. On the other hand, a bookie… oh yeah, they can take in a lot of cash."

Bruno remembered… Rick… yes, that was the gambler. He put rings around the paper every Saturday morning, and there'd be a row every Saturday night about how much money he'd lost. Eventually, he just went to races on Saturday and never came home. He wondered idly why his mum had so much bad luck picking men. Maybe they were all outsiders and long shots. Why didn't she go after one of the favorites instead?

"Well, nice ter meet ya, Tanner," he said, with half a smile, and he finished off his iced coffee.

CHAPTER THREE

The next morning, Tanner and Bruno were up with the others, ready to start clicking up their hours. The community vehicle known as the Jolly Bus collected them; its cartoon-covered sides spreading happiness and goodwill amongst anybody except the people inside. The replacement supervisor met them at Seven Plains, and they all signed in. Again, Bruno found Mrs. Dwyer watching for him as he approached.

"Good morning Bruno. How's the hand?"

Well, he had to answer, didn't he? So, he said with a shrug. "...T's okay, I guess. The nurse dressed it again yesterday."

"So... did you need a tetanus booster?"

"No, but they said to keep the dirt from getting into the wound."

"Well, that's okay. We can leave the rest of the vines for a bit while we sort out the bulbs."

Bruno thought to himself, "*What do you mean 'we'?*" But he just went to the garage door that wasn't a garage door and waited for Mrs. Dwyer to let him in. He walked around the back and observed his work from the day before. It was a mess! Soil that he had dislodged yesterday had been burrowed through somehow as if an angry rabbit had been evicted and his burrows torn open. And lying atop the mincemeat of a garden bed, Bruno could see ominous littler lumps of turds. "I didn't know you had pets," he said.

Mrs. Dwyer looked puzzled, then looked at the lumps and laughed. "Don't worry. I haven't. Those lumps are not what you think they are. They're bulbs. The maintenance man came around yesterday afternoon, and when he heard you'd been hurt, he ran the hoe over the dirt to loosen them for you."

Bruno blinked. Someone had done him a good turn. That was a first! "Ahh, tell him I said thanks," he muttered. Then, as an afterthought, "And thanks for showing Steve that glove yesterday. Did you tear it on purpose?"

Again Mrs. Dwyer laughed. "No, I used to wave it at an old crow to stop him scratching up my seedlings, and it caught on a broken wire on the clothesline. It was just providence that I hadn't thrown it out yet."

"Well, thanks anyway." He felt somehow that Mrs. Dwyer's action had made them some sort of partners in crime - though she was hardly a criminal for stretching the truth a bit. Still, it made him a little more affable, and he asked, "So, what's with the bulbs?"

"Oh! Well, we thought you might not be able to do much grabbing and pulling today," she answered, "so we can do the bulbs instead."

"Toss 'em in the green bin?" he asked.

Mrs. Dwyer shook her head. "Oh no! They're all fat with stored food for next year's flowers. We just put them in brown paper bags and label them, and plant them again in the new garden."

"Oh well, at least they're not gettin' chucked out like the snapdragons," he said as he grabbed a couple of bulbs.

Again Mrs. Dwyer shook her head. "They're all different kinds, you see, so we have to label the bags first."

Bruno's heart sank. "How will I know which are which?" He hated admitting his ignorance.

"Oh, we'll do it together. I can tell you what bulbs they are, and you can write the names on the paper bags. Then we'll pop them in the right bags. It's all ready in the kitchen." So, they went inside. Mrs. Dwyer had the kettle on and mugs ready for drinking. This time, he noticed she made him a coffee. She brought them from the bench to the table, where a stack of brown paper bags waited, with a fat texta alongside. Bruno hoped the spelling would be easy. "I can't hold the pen anymore," said Mrs. Dwyer, "and it's easy to confuse one bulb with another, so I got out Desmond's planting reference." She reached down on the spare chair and pulled up a black folder. It wasn't exactly a folder. It was a sort of papers carrier, the kind in movies that usually has 10, 000 dollars in it. "Desmond used it for work. When he retired, he kept all his gardening information in it. These are all the things he has grown, what has been removed, and what's there now." She handed Bruno the case, and with some hesitation, he slowly unzipped it. Inside, there was a drawing pad with a dark blue cover. On the opposite side were flaps that held pens and pencils in ridges, with a square patch for a rubber and a dent for a small glue-stick.

Bruno had never seen so many colored pencils! He'd had some at school, of course, a box of a dozen colors from The Reject Shop, but these were like rainbows of shades, with numbers on them, so you could see at a glance which one belonged where.

"Wow!" he said, "they look fantastic!"

Mrs. Dwyer smiled a little sadly. "Desmond loved drawing but never did it after he left school. Then, when his legs went on him, he took it up again and taught himself how to do it properly." She leaned over and flipped open the cover on the pad.

"GEEZ!" There was nothing else to say. On the table in front of him was a complete drawing of the garden in the backyard, just as it might have been before it went wild. The jasmine was snaking up its wire, while the happy wanderer clambered into the dark corner of the adjoining fences. The rosemary bent its lower branches down along the top row of bluestones in a thick carpet of blue flowers. Tall hollyhocks stood to attention along the back fence, with lime green euphorbia heads sprouting from their long stems of blue-green leaves. The little yellow roses, so abundant in the jungle outside, were fixed to wires that espaliered them in rows along the fence like golden notes written on a living page of music. Bruno couldn't count the number of different greens there were, and every plant was drawn with such accuracy that he could tell how many snapdragons had been planted in bright, colorful blobs all along the garden bed. Right at the front were the green sprouts that he knew were daffodils, and interspersed with them were the grassy leaves of another tiny plant with stems massed in purple pinheads. He pointed to these.

Mrs. Dwyer said, "Grape hyacinths." And pointing to another blue flower, then a pink one rather like a small waterlily, she said, "and these are hyacinths too, but not grape hyacinths. They're all the bulbs you saw lying around." She turned a few more pages of drawings and came to a list marked BULBS. There, Desmond had drawn the bulb and the flower of each plant he had placed in his precious garden.

Bruno couldn't believe his luck. He'd have no trouble labeling the paper bags now! He grabbed the texta and a bag and scrawled the word 'freesia' on it. The centers of each 'e' blended into a solid mass.

Mrs. Dwyer burst out laughing. "That looks like the eyes of a cartoon!" Embarrassed, Bruno turned the bag over and wrote more carefully on the other side. "Ah, that's much better. I can read it now." Bruno took a little more care than usual with the rest, and soon he had a dozen bags ready to accept their lumpy brown offerings.

They went back out to the turned-over garden bed. "So, the fat ones are the daffodils, yeah?" Bruno asked, picking up a couple of bulbs the size of onions.

"That's right, and the clumpy ones are the hyacinths. There are a lot of them."

"They look like underground cactus," Bruno said, examining the fleshy sections. "These other ones still have some flowers showing... the grapes?"

"Grape hyacinths. They make a lovely purple border just in front of the taller daffodils, like the King Alfreds."

"I thought daffodils were just daffodils; green leaves, yellow flowers."

"Oh my goodness, no! There are cream ones and white ones, and orange ones, even pale lime or pink!!" Mrs. Dwyer exclaimed. "Not ours. Ours are King Alfreds."

Bruno pulled a face of fake interest, but he was glad enough because he'd just written daffodils on the bag.

"There was a lady at one of the flats once. She had freesias in a pot. They made her flat smell real nice."

"Yes, they have a beautiful perfume. Desmond's freesias are along the ends, in the shade of the other bushes." Mrs. Dwyer picked out the drawing of the bulbous plant and showed him the bulbs. They looked like oversized pumpkin seeds. "These are freesias."

Bruno picked up a tiny brown root with a wilted green sprout emerging from it. "And what's this one?"

Mrs. Dwyer frowned. "Onion weed," she said flatly.

"Oh! Bin it?"

Mrs. Dwyer nodded emphatically. "Bin it!"

It didn't take all that long to sort out the bulbs and bag them up. Mrs. Dwyer produced a cardboard box to keep them in the dark. Then Bruno went along the turned soil picking free the small weeds and odd clover that had sneaked into the little plot. Once again, Mrs. Dwyer put the kettle on and put out some biscuits. Bruno thought she seemed to have a steady supply for someone who wasn't supposed to be eating biscuits. She had made tea again, but he didn't remind her that he drank coffee. The tea was good, to tell the truth, and he was more than ready for it.

As they sat, each wrapped in thought, Mrs. Dwyer put her head on one side in her hungry magpie way and said, "You know, you remind me of someone. Someone from years and years ago. I can't quite put my finger on it…"

Bruno shrugged. The comment held little interest for him. She didn't know him from Adam, and after this project was over, she wouldn't know him again. People who thought you reminded them of someone ended up identifying you in a line-up, because you reminded them of someone.

"His name was Zachary," she said, almost to herself. Then she repeated it, a little louder. "Zachary."

"Oh, a 'reffo'," Bruno nodded his head wisely.

"'Reffo?'"

"Yeah, you know, refugee. They all have names from the bible. Ezram or Joshua or Muzzletof."

Mrs. Dwyer looked at him strangely, then said, "Muzzletof is a greeting to wish you good fortune. It's not a name."

"Isn't it? There was a kid in the home, and this big kid always called him Muzzletof.

I thought it was his name!"

"Yiddish is the name of the language they use in Europe. They are Jews, and among themselves, they speak Jewish."

"Oh!" said Bruno. He had a feeling he was being told off, but he couldn't for the life of him think why.

"Anyway," Mrs. Dwyer was brisk now, "Zachary wasn't a 'reffo' and he wasn't a Jew. He was an Australian boy - probably around your age, maybe a year or two younger."

Bruno's eyes narrowed. *"She's fishing,"* he thought, *"just to find out how old I am."* Aloud he said, "Oh, so he was 18 or 19?"

Mrs. Dwyer just looked at him. There was no way Bruno was close to 20! "He was born into such love!" she said, smiling.

Bruno scowled. *"Yeah? Well, lucky him. I got work to do."*

He got up abruptly and took the small hoe, working through the loose soil until he had almost plowed the entire garden bed within an inch of its watering system. Bushes were listing, held in place by a few strands of roots. Tall stems leaned over flat against the ground, their root systems striving desperately to keep them upright. What was left of the climbers sagged against each other in tired submission as the ground beneath their feet sagged and separated into loamy handfuls of loose peat. Bruno worked his way along the path in silent fury as the thoughts swirled in his head. *"Bloody Zachary! Who cared about him anyway? So, he'd been born into such love. What of it? Probably some overfed, smarmy little snot who only had to smile at someone to get his every wish! Who needs a spoiled little smart-arse like that?"* He punched the hoe into the soil again, building up the image of the cute little toddler, dressed in his baby gear, being passed around his doting family. Was it anger or aching that engulfed him? Bruno didn't know. All he knew was that he didn't like Zachary.

"Stupid name for a skippy," he muttered. And suddenly, his anger spent itself, and he gave a short chuckle. He remembered an incident soon after he arrived at the children's home when some freckle-faced 'yobbo' had said much the same thing to him.

"Bruno? What kind of a name is that for an Aussie kid? You're a bloody wog!"

Bruno had laid him out on the spot and was sitting on his chest, pummeling his freckles when they dragged him off. *"I bet bloody Zachary would have run bawling to his mummy, and she'd have told ol' freckleface he was a naughty boy!"*

No-one ever teased Bruno about his name again. They just called him Bruiser instead. He liked it that way. Kids steered clear of him and left him to his own business. He spent the majority of his first months in that self-chosen isolation, and if sometimes he would have liked to make a peaceful overture, the other kids' hesitation soon brought the snarl back into his voice. Thus, he remained more or less a loner until he turned 15. When that birthday came around, marked by the usual cake and some small item of extra clothing, Bruno shrugged it off with 'who cares anyway?' But two things happened to make that year memorable for him. The first was that he was assigned a mentor to help him get ready to leave the home and find some kind of training or employment. He would be on a New Start allowance while he looked for work, but everyone knew that work was not readily available to kids with a problematic past.

His mentor, Rex, was a nice old codger who'd been around a bit. He seemed to have done many different things in his life, and he had books about people who lived interesting lives. There was one about Gulliver, who traveled to lands where the people were all small. At first, he'd refused to read such a fantasy until the old bloke had reminded him he liked *Planet of the Apes*, which was the same kind of fantasy; and that really, books like these let us see how other types of people ticked. So, he read it, and they spoke about the way people saw things. Then Rex brought in *Robinson Crusoe*, and they talked about his dependence on his Man Friday and the way Robinson Crusoe just assumed he was the boss because Man Friday was a native. They had long discussions about prejudice and pre-conceived ideas people had in their minds and didn't even know it. Bruno wasn't stupid. He knew he was supposed to learn lessons from the stories; lessons like how to get people to change their minds about the sort of person he was. Rex had probably been the only person in his life who had ever spoken to Bruno about such things. But Rex had a bad fall just a few weeks before Bruno left the home, and he went into care somewhere or another. Nobody told Bruno where he'd gone. That was part of the personal security setup. Bruno missed him.

The second thing that had happened was the arrival of a new kid at the home. There was a lot of secrecy about why he was there. He wasn't alone in the world, because he had visitors every Sunday. This lady used to come to see him, and she had her daughter with her. The girl was the first thing to draw Bruno's attention. It wasn't because she was pretty. He couldn't have told you what color her hair was or her eyes. No, what got to him was her sheer alive-ness. She was always looking around at everything, almost as if she were afraid she might miss something. Bruno hardly ever took any notice of his surroundings. Walls, spaces, seats, and food - that was all that interested him. A space that was his own, a seat at the table, food on the plate, what else was there?

The girl was different. She didn't look down at the floor and pretend not to see the scrabble of kids as she passed by. She looked right at them, invading their personal space, nodding at them if they caught her eye, or just smiling occasionally, as she had done to him. That smile had unsettled

Bruno. He had tried to scowl at her, but the scowl sort of curdled around the edges, and her smile suddenly became a big grin. Bruno dropped his eyes, but he found that he too was wearing a small smile.

The new kid was only there a few weeks while he saw a psychiatrist and some other medical types. But in those weeks, Bruno looked forward to the boy's visitors arriving almost as much as if they were his own visitors. And always, there would be that smile of recognition from the girl, and a corresponding response from Bruno; half-scowl, half-smile. Then the boy left with them, and there were no more visits. It was only later that Bruno discovered the story behind the little group. The boy had witnessed his father murder his mother. The lady was his mother's sister, and she had made arrangements to adopt the boy into her own family.

"Geez!" Bruno remarked to no-one in particular, "I'm glad it was him and not me!"

Bruno could remember more family arguments than he could family outings. They weren't always the same family group, though. His mum had gone through a few changes of partners, and although she always called them 'your new stepfather', Bruno knew well enough that none of them were his real father. When he'd asked her once, she just said, "Oh, he was no good. He didn't love you and he didn't love me," and she would say no more. But he could remember at least four semi-permanent stepdads, and eventually, his mother had quarreled with all of them.

With Rick, it had always been about money because he lost it all at the TAB. It was always the same, "It's my money. I earned it. Ain't no business of yours what I do with it!" Then it would be on for one and all. Rod was a different bucket of slime altogether. He'd dress himself up real flash and give her a smooth talk to come to the pub for a night out on the town. Rod took his mother from a happy, sometimes drunk mum, to a hopeless alcoholic. Bruno hated him for that and for all the other things he could add to the pile. Mum would say,

"What about the kid?" Bruno would know what was coming.

"Oh, nick in and fix it with the lady next door. We'll only be a couple of hours."

So, Bruno, bathed and in his pajamas, would sit on the couch with the lady next door or around the corner or up on the next landing watching whatever the oldies were watching until he fell asleep. He would still be there until lunchtime the next day, until gradually all the ladies refused to take him. "It ain't right for him to be still waitin' for yer until half-past one in the afternoon!" they would say, or "I'm sorry, luvvy but my hubby says I'm not allowed to take him anymore. It's makin' it too easy for you to dodge your responsibilities." It wasn't long after that they started putting him to bed and slipping out after they thought he'd gone to sleep. Of course, he didn't sleep. He'd lie stiff-legged in his bed, afraid to move in case the cold outside his own body warmth was some loathsome beast sliding its hand up to grab him. It took him hours to reach a state of exhaustion sufficient to fall asleep. That's when the bed-wetting began, and that's when Rod showed his true nature.

As soon as his mum set on him for the wet sheets, Rod would start to change color. It was a nauseating transformation. The skin on his forehead would start to mottle in patches of pink and fawn; the dark sunburned patches would grow darker, blending into shades of red and purple. Bruno's eyes would be transfixed as he stared at the vein in the side of Rod's neck. It pulsated like a thick piece of living string, trying to turn itself into the tip of a lash. Zorro had a lash, and this snaking, shaking line would be the end bit that curled and stung and slashed at you. Bruno never saw it escape, but he knew it did, because suddenly Rod would raise an arm and slap him across the face with such force that the boy would be lifted from the floor. He would have flown across the room had he not been held firm in the grasp of Rod's other hand. His screams were pathetic; all but drowned out by Rod's ranting, until they subsided into tiny whimpers like a beaten puppy, while his mum would stand there screeching at Rod to "Stop it! Lay of the kid for Chrissake! He won't do it again! Oh, Jesus, you're doing my head in!" But of course, he did do it again, and of course, so did Rod, and his mother was just as helpless to prevent it.

"Bruno!" He flinched before he realized it was not Rod, but Steve calling him. "Lunch break!"

He threw down the hoe and left without speaking to Mrs. Dwyer. The old bat had raked up too many memories with her bloody darling Zachary!

For her part, Mrs. Dwyer had a few thoughts of her own.

"Was Bruno the one?" She wondered. *"Could Bruno be the lead she needed to solve her private mystery?"*

CHAPTER FOUR

When Bruno returned from lunch, he had calmed down. He saw that the unit's door was closed, but the garage door was up, so he went around the back. The lady next door popped her head over the fence and said, "Mrs. Dwyer has just gone up to the office for a bit. She'll be back in a few minutes, so just go ahead. She's left you a drink on the step. I'm here if there are any problems." Bruno looked across and saw a large bottle of Coke sitting in a plastic container with some ice in it. Oh well, at least that was nice of her. He turned to the old chook from next door and decided to practice his charm. It didn't hurt to make a good impression, old Rex had said.

He gave her a wide, beaming smile. "Thanks, lady," he said, "It's nice to know where to turn to for help," and he made it sound as though he meant it.

The response was satisfying because the old dame smiled back and said, "It's always a pleasure to help someone with good manners!" and then she disappeared.

With a much smaller smile to himself, Bruno started work. He decided to finish off the standing vines and yanked with the hoe. Even though half the soil had been loosened, the vines refused to pull free. He hacked at the soil with the hoe and tried again. Still, he could not budge the tangle of ropey roots that clung to the soil below. He dug again - and again, yet, the vines would not pull free. In the end, he grabbed a shovel from the corner and hopped up onto the garden. His head was now above the fence, and he could see into the gardens on either side and the walkway that meandered around the backs of the homes. Skirting a bowling green and a closed fernery, the 'garden' was neatly set out with an occasional tallish tree, separated by small bushes in perfect order, and matching in height.

"Huh!" he sneered. "That ain't a real garden! You should take a look in here! This garden is doing its own thing!"

"I agree entirely!" said a voice behind him, and he got such a shock he nearly fell off the garden. He dug the shovel in just in time to stop himself.

"I'm sorry, Bruno." Mrs. Dwyer looked at him anxiously. "I didn't mean to startle you. I did ask the lady next door to explain."

Bruno tried to recover his composure. "It's okay. She did let me know. I was just talking to myself."

Mrs. Dwyer looked relieved. "Oh, I do that all the time!" she said, reverting to her normal pleasantry. "It's the only way I can guarantee an intelligent audience!"

Bruno laughed despite himself. "Yeah! Good one," he said, jumping down from his perch. "I was getting out the vines, but it's much harder than I thought."

"Well, most plants have a root system just as big as their canopy," Mrs. Dwyer was matter of fact, so Bruno didn't mind asking the question.

"Canopy?"

In return, Mrs. Dwyer pointed to one of the larger trees outside. "All the branches and leaves make up the canopy."

Bruno looked at the vines, doing a quick calculation of how much canopy there might be all together. "Shit!" he said without thinking, "I'll have to dig a bloody cave!"

Mrs. Dwyer shook her head. "You can cut through the roots with the shovel. Then you can heave out the main vine. Without the canopy, the root system will gradually shrivel."

Bruno looked at the vigorous vines thoughtfully. "Seems a shame that we have to kill everything that's growing so good."

"If we don't cut the taproot, the vine can be transplanted. And even if we do, sometimes the vines can be grafted on to another living plant."

"I've heard of that. I remember once I saw an apple tree that had pears on it! It was a children's farm or somewhere."

"Yes, there are plants that take grafting well, especially fruit trees."

"I thought it was weird," he said, quite enjoying the conversation to his surprise.

"Not much different to kids being grafted into a new family," she said carefully, watching to see the effect of her words.

"Yeah, I heard about that too. The only one I saw though was a kid who went to live with his aunty. I never knew anyone who wasn't with some part of their family."

"Desmond was adopted outside of his family. He was an only child, though. He didn't have any brothers or sisters."

"Like me," said Bruno, giving away a single thread of information. He decided to change the subject. "Thanks for leaving out the Coke. I might have some now." He reached for the Coke, and she held out a paper bag towards him.

"I picked up a couple of these at the food bar," she said.

Bruno put in his hand and drew out an apple pastry. His face brightened. "Yum!" he said and took a bite.

Mrs. Dwyer smiled. "I'm not supposed to eat these either, but some rules are made to be broken, don't you think?"

Bruno nodded, grinning. He'd been breaking most rules all his life! With the bucket and Coke gone from the step, Mrs. Dwyer sat down, and the two ate their snacks in more or less comfortable silence. After a while, she said, "Desmond had a bad start to life, you know, and some people were afraid that he would never overcome his problems, but his new family helped him to sort out his priorities."

Bruno stiffened a little. "I got my priorities sorted," he said with some defensiveness. "Get these hours worked off, and then disappear. Go interstate maybe, where no-one has ever heard of me."

"Good plan at your age. Have you lined up work that you like to do?"

"I'll cross that bridge when I come to it."

"Oh, I didn't mean to pry. I'm just interested because I have some connections interstate. If you're into farming, my cousin grows strawberries near Cleveland in Queensland. They always want pickers in the season."

Bruno stored this information and then said, "I thought I might do something with cars."

"Hm. My nephew did panel beating for a bus company. But he had to go to school in Melbourne somewhere, where they taught all the automotive trades."

"I'll be training on the job," said Bruno firmly. He'd need a working pay packet to pay for accommodation and food. Rex had taught him all about that. Start with unskilled laborer jobs, save a little, and then transfer to a job where training was part of the salary package. That was the way to get ahead. Right now though, just finding a job - any job -was the problem.

"I see," she said, deciding not to explore further.

It was not the time to ask for clues.

"I hope everything works out well for you, Bruno," she said. Bruno nodded, and a small glow warmed him because he knew - he knew without a doubt that the old doddy really meant it. When he returned home that night, Bruno felt very relaxed, as if he'd had a bit of good luck. Of course, it didn't have anything to do with Mrs. Dwyer. She was nothing but a silly old lady, maybe a bit kinder than some, but of no account to him. Nevertheless, he walked with a bit of a spring in his step, and young Tanner noticed it as soon as he walked into the living room.

"Well, you're looking chirpy! How's the hand?"

Bruno hadn't given his hand a thought, yet now it registered that it was a bit sore. "Gettin' better. Nothin' keeps me down for long." He looked at Tanner, noticing he was dressed for outside. He must have done his hours today.

"Guts okay now?"

"Yer," said Tanner, dropping his eyes a bit too quickly, and Bruno knew he was still feeling a bit off. Too tough to let it show, though!

Bruno decided this was a stand he understood and nodded. "Might still need to take it easy for a coupla' days. Never can tell with gut bugs." Tanner nodded and relaxed. Bruno studied him for a moment longer. He realized that 'young Tanner' was the wrong term. There was something in the boy's face that told Bruno he was not much younger at all, possibly even the same age as himself. Maybe he just had a little more innocence, if this was his first community order?

"Not my business," he murmured to himself, but before he left the room, he tossed Tanner a magazine he'd picked up from a seat in the village. "Here," he said off-handedly, "I've finished with it."

"Oh, thanks!" Tanner said, and he grabbed the magazine with such enthusiasm that Bruno was surprised.

"If you like readin' em, I can get more," he offered.

"That'd be great!" said Tanner, smiling openly now. "I love reading all the new ideas that are happening everywhere, so I'll know what kind of training I should apply for."

"Just apply for a job where they train you." Bruno shrugged. "What could be easier?"

But Tanner shook his head. "Nah. If I do that, they get to control what I learn to do. I want to control what I learn so that I can decide for myself what kind of job I want."

Bruno shook his head. "Man, they're not for our kind. We gotta pay the landlord. We take any job we can get!"

Tanner shook his head in return. "I made it through year nine before I goofed off. If I go back to this new kinda school they're talkin' about, and if I can last until I get to year 11, I can apply for a trade apprenticeship."

Bruno shrugged. "Then go for it!" he said as he walked away. Year 11! He'd bombed out in year seven and wagged school nearly all of year eight. No new kinda school was gonna do him any good. But a little thought niggled at the back of his mind. When he was in year seven, he couldn't read correctly, and he couldn't work out the math quickly enough. Well, he was still slow at math but he mostly came up with the right answers. But he could read okay now, so maybe he didn't bomb-out in year seven after all. Maybe the year seven that he happened to be in bombed-out on him?

He brushed the thought out of his mind and went looking for something to eat. After dinner, he watched TV and found one of the supervisors there to give them some kind of talking to. It wasn't Steve this time. It was a guy called Zarb. He never did know his full name. Zarb had more tattoos than he had skin left to draw them on, but the boys knew he was an okay sort of bloke. Zarb got their attention and said quietly, "There's a show on TV tonight that I really want you guys to see, and if you have questions afterward, I've got some answers ready." The boys gave each other that 'do I have a choice here?' look, and Zarb turned on the ABC.

The show was interviewing people - kids and teachers alike, about why this school was doing such a good job with their problem students. A few of the boys rolled their eyes, but when the kids started talking about how low they'd been and how great they felt now, even Bruno got interested. It wasn't as if they were 'super brats' or anything. One worked weekends at a small supermarket cleaning up. Another helped out at the local garage on Friday nights and Sunday afternoons. One of them had even left school altogether for a year and a half and then come back! *Why would anyone want to do that?"* Bruno asked himself.

But the thing that got him was that these kids all admitted they had been really bad students. They failed most of their exams, played truant on test days, swore at the teachers, and picked fights in the schoolyard! All of that, Bruno could identify with. What he couldn't reconcile was these neat and tidy kids, clean clothes ironed - by themselves mostly - who sat there saying, "This time I wanted to be there. I wanted to be successful, and when I told the teachers that, they bent over backward to help me!" No school Bruno ever went to made him feel like that! He sat there silent as Zarb switched off the TV.

"I know most of you guys had a shit time at school, and I'm not asking any questions about your grades. This school they're talking about works on the idea that people are more important than grades and marks. They are talking to other schools to bring them across to their way of thinking."

"Yeah, like where, Canberra?" The comment raised a laugh, but it quickly died as Zarb shook his head.

"The thing is, they'd like to try a school like this, right here, if they get enough inquiries. There's an old primary school that's been closed down for a couple of years, right up behind the Seven Plains Aged Care Facility."

"I know that place!" It was Tanner who spoke. "When it was running, the little kids had a school veggie plot." He paused, looking a bit embarrassed. "I used to nick in and raid it when I was hungry."

"But that's for little kids," objected another boy.

"That's who it used to be for." Zarb corrected him. "What they are doing now is offering two years of a school experiment for first offenders."

"Well, that lets me out!" thought Bruno. Somewhere inside, he felt a sting of relief or was it regret?

"Tanner said anyone could go!" protested another.

"This is my second community order, so I'll miss out!" Zarb smiled.

"Actually, Tanner was right! When they say 'first offenders', they mean anyone whose sentence was not inside a jail cell. As long as you have only had community orders, you will be eligible to go back to school and have a crack at passing. BUT..." he warned, "and this is a big but... you really have to want to be there. If you don't really want to be there, then they'll give your place to somebody who does!"

Tanner was the first to stand up. "I want that chance Zarb," he said, as clear as clear. "I want that chance! Everyone knows timers are the last ones in the job queue. I want a real 'new start'! I reckon I can pass if I don't have any..." He paused then said, "domestic upheavals."

Bruno wondered what domestic upheavals Tanner had experienced. He seemed pretty calm most of the time. Every time Bruno thought about domestic upheavals, they seemed to churn him up until he was mad enough to smash something. Suddenly he remembered that pulsing vein in Rod's neck. *"Did he have a vein like that?"* he wondered, *"Would he turn into a turd like Rod and smash little kids' faces?"*

Something in him recoiled sharply from the thought. He needed to be tough to survive, and he knew that. But he did NOT want to grow up and turn into a cruel bastard like Rod! Unless he did something drastic, he might very well be on that path already! He couldn't stomach the thought that he might rage out of control until he smashed some little kid like that!

He pulled away from his thoughts. A couple of the other boys were hesitating but asking questions.

"Will we have to do homework? I fill shelves at night when I'm not, you know."

"There is homework, but you can negotiate everything. That's part of the policy; to work with where you are at in your lives. They place your needs first and keep the rules second."

"Can you sign on for a couple of months to try it out?" asked another. Zarb shook his head.

"Afraid not. That makes it too easy to opt-out, and you've wasted a chance for somebody else. You have to sign on for two full years."

"Hey! The year's already started!" said another. "We'll be behind before we start!"

No, you won't," explained Zarb. "Each boy is on his own course, so he gets individual tuition until he's ready to link up with someone else on the same level. Even if there's no-one else on your level, you start when you start, and you finish when you achieve that year's pass mark."

"Even if you take two years to do one year?" asked another.

Zarb nodded.

"Say something worked out well, and you wanted to go the whole high school thing? Like, try for year 11 or 12?"

"Then I guess they'd call the experiment a success and open year 11 and 12," said Zarb. "Or maybe you'd move into a regular school."

From the grunts and sour faces, Zarb could see that the idea of regular school didn't appeal at all.

"How would we pay for our rent and food?" asked Bruno. "We ain't got no parents to support us!"

"They've thought of that. There is a pension called the Double Orphan Pension for kids who have no parent. The government is looking into that as a means of support. You'd still be living in shared accommodation, exactly like this, but going to school instead of doing community service orders."

"Would we have a supervisor checking us in and out?" Tanner asked.

Zarb grinned. "No need!" he said. "The school does its own roll call, and if you're not there - unless you have a bloody good reason, you're out of the project."

There was silence for a few minutes, and then two more boys said they'd like to sign on. Zarb looked at them. Three of the others would return to parents and a regular school as soon as their hours were up. It was the long-term truants that he really wanted to encourage.

"What about you, Bruno? You still have time to make changes in your life. Think about aiming a bit higher, maybe?"

"Changes in his life! Hadn't he just made up his own mind to do that? Still, it wouldn't do to just fall in too easy with these do-gooders."

"I'll think about it," he said, carefully casual. "I'll let ya know my decision tomorrer night."

CHAPTER FIVE

The next morning Bruno slept late. He had done a bit of tossing and turning, so he was grumpy as well. It didn't help that most of the best breakfast choices were finished. So, he ate a quick bowl of fairly tasteless cereal and hurried out just as the Jolly Bus pulled up.

By the time he arrived at Mrs. Dwyer's, he was ready for an argument. As soon as he saw her waiting on her little porch, he felt the fuses burn.

"Good morning, Bruno," she said with a smile.

"Mornin'," he mumbled.

Mrs. Dwyer's smile disappeared at once. "Oh dear, is something wrong? Your hand isn't playing up is it?"

"No, it isn't!" he growled. "Why are you always checkin' up on me? That I get here on time. What's it to you if I'm late, or my hand is sore? I don't mean nuthin' to you, and you don't mean nuthin' to me!"

Mrs. Dwyer's eyebrows shot up almost to her hairline. This was not the response she had expected. "I'm not checking up on you, Bruno. I know the Jolly Bus delivers you," she explained. "I stand out here every morning until my friend at number 12 comes out and stands on her verandah. That way, we both know we're alright. It's keeping an eye out for each other. You just happen to arrive at the same time. It's a coincidence, that's all."

Bruno felt his face grow hot. He hated being embarrassed, and he sure did feel that way right now. "Well… I thought…" Bruno started.

Mrs. Dwyer continued, "And I am concerned about your hand because it happened while you were helping me. Of course, I'd be concerned about any of my friends."

"We ain't friends!" Bruno blurted. "I'm just a timer on community orders. I'm just clockin' up hours. In two more weeks, we'll all be finished here, and then you'll never see me again."

"Anyone who helps me, I consider a friend," said Mrs. Dwyer calmly, "If we never do meet again, I will always tell people I had a friend once, whose name was Bruno and he helped me sort out Desmond's garden."

Bruno felt his anger dissolve as her calm words settled him down. "I'm only doin' time here," he said, in a much calmer tone now. "That ain't like bein' a friend."

"We're all doing time here, Bruno," she smiled gently. "Every last one of us. It isn't the time that is the sentence; it's how you feel about what you're doing with that time."

Bruno looked at her with some puzzlement. "Time's time," he said. "Clock up the hours. Get it over with."

Mrs. Dwyer shook her head. "Not really. If that were all there was, we'd all just clock up hours until we die. What's the point in that? If you spend those hours really loving what you're doing, you stop counting them and they go by so fast, you can't believe it!"

Bruno didn't believe her for a minute. Gettin' through the day, that was it; finding some way to make the hours pass, gettin' a feed, grateful for a warm bed. Every day was a struggle. He said that now. "Ya just gotta get through the day. That's it! I gotta get on with it." And he walked to the garage door, waiting while she opened it.

Today he was back up on the raised bed, cutting around the vine's root ball with the edge of his spade. After a few minutes, he got the hang of the angle he needed and found that he was slicing through them with a single shear. It was much better than hacking at them with the side of the blade; soon he was working his way around the accessible sides, cutting clean slices at even distances all around the root ball. Then he started to lever the stubborn things out of the ground.

He knew he had to keep the taproot complete if the vines were to be re-planted. So, he levered carefully under the root ball, gauging how much to wriggle the spade and when to ease off. He was relieved when the first vine came loose, and a happy wanderer fell over sideways, its taproot exposed and complete. "No wonder they call it a taproot," he muttered to himself, "It's as thick as a bloody water-pipe!"

"Well done!" said Mrs. Dwyer, who suddenly appeared with coffee and a plate of the forbidden biscuits.

Bruno was surprised. "Is it coffee time already? I only just started."

"You've been wrestling with that vine for nearly two hours," said Mrs. Dwyer. "How time flies when you're having fun!"

Bruno had the good sense to acknowledge the dig. "Well, I don't know if I'd call it fun, but I sure did get stuck into it, so maybe you're right. Some times go faster than others."

"Coffee time goes fast too, so you'd better drink this while it's still hot!" She put the coffee and biscuits on the back step, went back inside, and came out with a little folding table. She put the things on the table.

"Desmond used to use this when he took his sketch pads into the bush."

Bruno frowned. "How could he get that wheelchair into the bush? Wouldn't he need a paved pathway or something?"

Mrs. Dwyer shrugged. "He used to hire a special one for the day, and a man always went with him in case it tipped over. The wheelbase was much narrower."

Bruno understood the dynamics involved and was impressed that someone had invented such a thing. "Must be lots of things like that you could make for people who are… you know…"

"Disabled? Oh yes, there's a shop in Bendigo where you can get all kinds of aids. My kettle tips itself over for me without spilling."

"Who invents them?"

"Mechanics, engineers, plumbers, electricians, computer scientists, anybody really, with a bit of technical know-how."

Bruno gave that some thought. "A bit of technical know-how eh? I'm pretty good at working out how things work, like mechanical things, not electricity or computers."

Mrs. Dwyer gave him a thoughtful glance but kept the conversation easy. "Oh, bikes… clocks, things like that?"

"Yeah. Even at the home… school," he amended quickly, "it was me that fixed the hinges on the guinea pig cage. Stuff like that."

"I guess you must have a mechanical mindset." She picked up the coffee mug and the plate and turned to go back inside.

Bruno cleared his throat and she waited. He could never say afterward why he decided to confide in her. It just happened. "They're offering some of us a chance to go back to school - a new kind of school where they give ya extra help."

"That's a pretty big decision to make when you have to take care of yourself. Will they support you financially?"

"Yeah. Somethin' called the Double Orphan Pension."

"Well, that's a plus! At least it gives you some choices."

"Choices?"

"Well, yes. I mean if you go into the workforce with..." Mrs. Dwyer paused. "...whatever skills you have now, you'll get by - once you land a job - because you are a good worker. You're not lazy. If you can get some on-the-job training, that's even better."

"Yeah, that's what I've been thinkin'."

"If you went back to this school with the extra help, then even if you only did it for one year and did the same things, your starting wage would be more because of the extra year of school."

Bruno was surprised. "Would it?"

"Oh yes. A junior with year 12 gets about three dollars an hour extra in his pay than a junior with year..." she hesitated again, guessing "...10."

Bruno did not tell her that he didn't even have year nine. But he looked crestfallen.

Mrs. Dwyer felt sorry for him. "The school would have a careers advisor. They'd give you all the up-to-date stuff about apprenticeships and jobs like that."

Bruno said in a low voice, "Eric and Tanner told me you had to have year 11 to get an apprenticeship."

Mrs. Dwyer wondered who Eric and Tanner were, but she just nodded. "That's mostly true, but sometimes there are companies that will take on an apprentice with a special interest, like for instance, animal care at the zoo, or personal carers for kids in wheelchairs. They do a special course. It's pretty tough; lots of paperwork and forms to understand."

"They'll only take you at this school if you really, truly want to be there, to go back to school and have another go at changing your future." Bruno said, adding with some desperation, "I gotta tell 'em tonight what I decided."

Mrs. Dwyer felt his dilemma and wondered what to tell him. Finally, she said, "Well only you know what line you're on right now, Bruno. You can draw a straight line from what got you this far, and your mind can draw a line that tells you where it's going to take you."

Bruno was pretty sure he didn't need to imagine any such thing. He was already dreading a future that would turn him into another Rod!

"Or," Mrs. Dwyer continued, "you can use your mind to imagine where you might be if you make this decision tonight. It's your choice."

"Yeah," said Bruno, "I know." He picked up his spade and clambered back up onto the raised garden bed. "I'm sorry I snarled at you this morning."

Mrs. Dwyer nodded. "You had a lot on your mind," she said quietly and went inside. As she washed the things up, she made a decision of her own. In two weeks, Bruno had said they'd be finished here. She would have to ask him tomorrow. She knew she was not supposed to ask the boys any personal questions, but how else was she to find out anything? She would need time to follow any leads. Ready or not, she would ask him tomorrow.

Steve came around early that afternoon. They took the Jolly Bus around past the old primary school, so the boys could get some idea of the public transport available. The public bus that dropped the oldies off after their pension day shopping went on past the proposed new park and terminated at the school. It was the end of the line. The phrase was lost on Bruno as he looked at the cluster of buildings. "*There are no shops for us to get to*", he thought. "No *point in leaving the school grounds.*" Down at the far end, they could see workers setting up cricket nets, and there was a truck delivering concrete just backing up.

Tanner took the seat next to him. "Well, the buildings are in better shape than I thought they'd be!" he said. "I expected it to be trashed by now."

Bruno nodded. "They probably were. A lot of the paintwork looks pretty new. Some of the schools I went to were old dungeons; freezing cold in winter, and so old that the windows wouldn't open in summer."

Tanner grinned. "Yer wouldn't want to smell what might drift in where I was. It was just down the road from the abattoirs."

Bruno was not usually tender about such things, but today he felt his guts squirm. "Ya gotta wonder why people live in places like that."

"Cheap," said Tanner. "Work."

Thinking of the animals, Bruno said hesitatingly, "What kinda work?"

"One of my mum's boyfriends was a slaughterman."

"Oh."

"There was another bloke, a bit of a sleaze, y'know? He was an auctioneer. Made a bit of money, but geez, what a pathetic piece of shit he was!" Bruno nodded. He didn't want any explanations. He'd never bothered much about what people thought of him. What was the point? But now, he decided that he didn't want people to think he was a piece of shit either.

When he'd started fighting back, people said he was a mean little brat and that he'd be better off when somebody cut him down to size. "Well, let'em try!" he whispered. "I can take care of myself!"

Tanner heard the second half and responded. "Yeah, I mean a guy's a guy. Ya gotta fight back somehow. Only for my mum, it was different."

"How come?" asked Bruno. "They can be just as bad! "

"My mum needed a leader," Tanner said, "When she was a kid, her mum had told her, 'Always find the leader. He's the one who'll take care of you.'"

"Oh." Bruno hadn't heard anything like that. "Trouble was," Tanner confided, "she always picked wannabe leaders, not real leaders. Then they spent the rest of the time bragging about how they were top dog."

Bruno thought about Rod. "Yeah. I know the type."

Tanner suddenly became confidential. "That's why I wanna get back to school and see if I can go right through. I don't wanna have people starin' at me like I'm a piece o'shit. I got a good brain - I think. I was real quick with the bookies, odds-on and everything. I reckon I can pass at math, and I can read and write pretty good. Yer hafta be careful about spelling the horses' names and write 'em clear so they can read 'em properly. Well, hell, I can do that!"

Bruno was surprised at his enthusiasm but just nodded as Tanner warmed up. "But mostly I wanna find out things; things I don't know yet! I wanna find out why some people think university is important. I wanna see the right way to do experiments. I wanna know why some people seem to sail through life real easy and why other people like me - and you," he added, "get the splintery end of the stick."

Bruno could identify with that last bit. "Yeah," he said, "the splintery end of the stick."

Tanner stopped ranting. He slumped back. "Anyway, that's why I'm going back to school."

Bruno was silent. He couldn't remember anyone ever telling him that school was the place to find out stuff like that. He'd been to six or seven different schools, and as far as he could see, they were pretty much all the same.

"Yah! Yah! Can't even read yet!"

This idea of being able to find out real stuff was different. It gave Bruno a lot to think about. He tried to imagine what it would be like to actually want to go to school, to find out interesting stuff, to see what made the world tick. And what about science experiments? He wasn't sure about them. "Maybe I could learn to weld. That'd help me get a good job!" Then his mind drew the line for him, and he saw his name on a little repair shop, panel beaters, or maybe a spare parts yard, where he could fix panels and sell 'em second hand. Maybe he could change his life! He was lost in thought all the way home and pretty quiet at the dinner table.

Later that evening, Zarb came up to him quietly and said, "Well Bruno, have you given any thought to your decision?"

For a moment, an image flashed across his mind; that of sitting in a cell for hours and hours every day. "Shit!" he said aloud, "I still got a choice!" Zarb's relief was enormous, when Bruno said, "Well, I don't fancy spendin' two years behind bars if I stuff up again, so I'm gonna give myself those two years to try this new school; to really get stuck into it, and…" He paused and took a deep breath, and with the tiniest hint of vulnerability in his eyes, he said rather gruffly, "if they're gonna help sort me out with the tough bits, I will give it everything I've got. Maybe I do want a new kinda future."

The whisper went round the place in no time. "Bruno's gonna go back to school!"

And in some places, the next sentence was, "No shit? Well, if he can do it, maybe I can too!"

CHAPTER SIX

Bruno's decision didn't make any difference to his here and now, though, so the next morning, he was back at Mrs. Dwyer's on time, and Mrs. Dwyer was out there again. But this time, Bruno noticed the lady in number 12 also standing on her porch. "Good morning Bruno," she said.

"*Oh Geez*," he thought, "*now I gotta be polite to two of 'em!*" Nevertheless, he looked up and turned on a reasonable cheerful expression. "Good mornin', missus."

"Mrs. Schmidt." Where had he heard that tone before?

"Mrs. Schmidt," he added.

"That's good." The old duck nodded like a carnival puppet. "A person's name makes them a somebody, not a nobody!" And she gave a squeaky cackle.

Bruno laughed at the sound rather than the words, but he was still smiling when Mrs. Dwyer saw him and said, "Great to see you looking happy, Bruno! That smile lights up your whole face!"

Immediately he tried to wipe the smile off his face, but somehow it just stayed there. Anyway, he felt pretty good, so what of it? "Yeah, well, it's gonna be a good day. I got the trick o' them vines now, and they won't beat me again." Mrs. Dwyer ducked back inside and opened the garage door for him. He didn't waste any time talking this morning but grabbed the spade and started slicing through the roots of the jasmine.

Mrs. Dwyer looked a bit disappointed but said nothing.

"Why on earth did I think this stuff was easy?" he wondered, as tangle after tangle of the wiry tendril bounced away from his spade and sprang back again, refusing to cut through. In the end, he pinned them down with the spade while he cut through them with the secateurs. Finally, he cleared a complete circle around the main stem and started levering out the root ball.

Again, he was surprised to hear Mrs. Dwyer's voice. "Do you want your coffee now, or after you get that out?" He turned around, just as the root ball came clear, and the next thing he knew he was on his backside, clutching at the vines to stop himself from falling. "Oh, I'm so sorry! I didn't mean to startle you!" she cried in alarm.

"Yer didn't," Bruno said as he tried to regain his composure, "That bloody jasmine did, comin' loose right then like that!"

If Mrs. Dwyer noticed that he'd sworn, she didn't show it. She just put the things on the little folding table and said, "Do you want to wash up first?"

Bruno was about to say no. Then he caught sight of his gloves. They were caked in mud. "I'll just take the gloves off," he said and pulled them off quickly, but his fall had scooped a good handful of mud into each glove, so in the end, he said, "I'd better." He went into the tiny bathroom and cleaned up. When he came out, Mrs. Dwyer was in the kitchen, obviously waiting for him. He checked to see if he'd left a mud trail, then looked at her.

She seemed to be holding her breath. "Bruno, I need to ask you something. I hope you won't mind?"

Instantly his guard went up. "Depends on what it is," he said quietly.

"It's about your name. Is Bruno your real name?" His defenses were on the rise now. "They told us you were all warned not to ask nosey questions."

The old doddy was getting agitated now. "I know, and I'm sorry, but I do have a serious reason for asking."

"Well… not that it's any of your business… but yeah, it is. My dad's family came out from Italy after World War One, and my great grandfather was a war hero, so they called me after him." None of it was true, except for the fact that Bruno was his real name.

All the tension went out of her. In fact, to Bruno's horror, she looked as if she might cry. "So even if the boys don't give us their right names, the supervisors know them?"

"Geez!" he thought. *"Is Mrs. Dwyer stupid or something?"* But he answered curtly... "Of course they do. The names are on our charge sheets. But they won't tell you anyway. There are privacy laws ya know!"

If Mrs. Dwyer thought it odd that he should claim the protection of a law, she didn't say so. Instead, she said, "I know they won't. I asked that supervisor - Steve? He said it was restricted information."

Bruno frowned. It would look bad on his report if she wanted to report him. "Why would you wanna report me? I ain't broken anythin' or pinched anythin'!" he stopped when he remembered his temper outburst.

But Mrs. Dwyer was shaking her head. "Oh no, it was nothing like that! I thought that... I was hoping you might help me. You see, I just have to find Zachary. I just have to."'

Bruno's eyes almost popped out of his head.

"Lady, we ain't the Lost Boys' Home. Why in hell would ya be expectin' Steve or me to help ya find Zachary? He's probably pooncin' around at the bloody university, livin' the high life and chattin' up them toffee-nosed bit..." He quickly he re-phrased, "...bits of skirt."

"No, he isn't," Mrs. Dwyer answered sadly. "The last I heard, he was in a detention center."

The silence was like a living thing in the room. Bruno was struck dumb, but his mind was racing. Zachary? The star of the 'happy family'? Zachary in a detention center! That meant he was in deeper shit than Bruno was. He must'a done some pretty serious stuff.

"Geez!" he finally whispered. "What'd he do?"

"He burned a house down."

Bruno let his breath out with a whoomph. He hadn't even noticed he was holding it. "Was anybody hurt?" He didn't want to say killed.

Mrs. Dwyer also heaved a sad sigh. "No, but they decided he was a danger to the community and to himself, and they locked him up. I've been looking for him for such a long time."

"Well, his family will know. I mean, if he's my age, they'll have all his details, and when his time's up, he'll go back to his family."

"No, that's the problem, you see. I promised Zachary's grannie he could come to me when he came out, and I'd help him start again. But he'll be a young man like you, and I won't know him. So, I have to find him before he finishes his sentence."

Bruno couldn't work this out at all. "I don't understand. This kid had such a loving family. Why would he come to you? I ain't bein' rude or nothin', but they usually reckon old grandmothers aren't much good at controllin' tearaway kids. They'd send him back to his parents."

"They're all gone," said Mrs. Dwyer heavily. "Everyone who ever loved him... all gone. And he will spend his whole life thinking no-one ever loved him, and it's not his fault. It was never his fault."

Privately, Bruno thought to himself, *"Well, burnin' down the house was his fault!"* but he had a feeling that Mrs. Dwyer wasn't really talking about that.

She was talking again. "When I knew you were about his age, I thought maybe you had heard of him... I even wondered if you might be him, but you're not, of course."

Bruno felt that flush of resentment rise. It wasn't his bloody fault. He was Bruno, and bad luck if that was a disappointment to her. Bugger her anyway. "No, I'm not!" he said abruptly and went back outside. He picked up the coffee, but it was barely warm, and, pulling a face, he swallowed it down in a gulp. Grabbing the spade, he slammed it down on the jasmine and sliced the tap root clean off. "Fuck!" he snarled, but his anger started to dissipate. "It wasn't the jasmine's fault either," he muttered,

"Shit just happens." And he went on working with a little less vehemence.

Just before lunch, Mrs. Dwyer came out, and he could see she'd been crying.

"Bruno," she said in a quiet voice, "I didn't mean to offend you about not being Zachary. I was just disappointed that I couldn't get a lead somehow. In one way, I'm really glad you're not Zachary because you have proved to me that there are good young men caught up in the struggles of life. Not all of us start with the same advantage, but your brush with the law has not stopped you from being honest, industrious, and reliable. You have given me hope that Zachary might be able to turn his life around too. You see, he's carrying the blame. Everybody blamed him. He doesn't understand that things were going wrong even before he was born. That's what I need him to know, that it wasn't all his fault!"

Bruno didn't hear much about Zachary. He did hear that he, Bruno, was a good young man; that he was honest, industrious, and reliable. He didn't know whether the old doddy had finally cracked up, or if she was talking about somebody else. Because he muttered to himself, "If that's what she sees in me, then she needs new glasses!"

As he stood there half-listening to her, he realized that she had another little bit of truth in her words. *"You know what,*

Bruno?" he said to himself, *"It wasn't all your fault either. You didn't fuck up your life all by yourself!"* And with that realization, a load shifted somewhere inside him. The angry retort 'It's not my fault!' wasn't a defensive snarl anymore. It was a simple, self-evident truth. He looked down at her from his perch on the raised garden, suddenly feeling very tall and knowing and kindly disposed towards this peculiar old lady. "It's okay Mrs. Dwyer. I understand you've had a lot on your mind."

She gave him a watery smile. "Your coffee went cold. I'll make you a fresh one." He nodded and levered out the yellow climbing roses.

After lunch, they bagged up the vines and roses that Bruno had dug up. He felt a bit bad about the jasmine. Mrs. Dwyer was quick to point out, there was another one in the far corner. They would still have one for the garden. The maintenance man said he'd break up the root clump and see if some rootstock would take. That made Bruno feel a bit better, and the afternoon flew past in quiet, companionable work. When they finally stood up and removed their gloves, the maintenance man slapped Bruno across the shoulders with his gloves and said,

"Good job, Lad. It's been a pleasure working with you…"

"Bruno."

"Yes, well, good job, Bruno!" He turned to walk away. "See you again."

"That Mrs. Schmidt was right, Bruno thought, *a person with a name is a somebody, not a nobody."*

He turned to Mrs. Dwyer's single rose bush, surrounded by the bagged vines.

"Hey, you lot! My name's Bruno, and I'm a good young man! I'm honest, industrious, and reliable!" And he said it with such vigor that he almost believed it for a moment or two.

Mrs. Dwyer came out at the sound of his voice, but she obviously hadn't heard what he said. "Thank you very much for all your hard work today Bruno." She looked uncertain. He wished she'd eye him off again like a hungry magpie. He liked that little bit of cheek in her.

"Oh, you ain't got rid o' me yet," he said airily. "I'll be back termorrer." She did smile then, and he was surprised at how relieved he felt. He tossed his gloves onto the porch railing and waved goodbye as he sauntered back to sign off.

Mrs. Dwyer looked after him as he walked away. The smile left her face, and she whispered, "Oh Zachary, you poor lonely boy. I don't think I'll ever be able to find you!"

CHAPTER SEVEN

It was only the next morning that Bruno realized he hadn't told Mrs. Dwyer about his decision to go back to school. He wondered why it mattered, yet somehow it did. He wanted her to know that he was more than she knew him to be. It was a long time since he felt that way towards anyone. Now he wanted someone to care that he'd chosen a new direction. As he walked down to Mrs. Dwyer's, he saw that Mrs. Schmidt was out on her verandah.

"This'll give her a shock," he thought to himself, grinning, as he called out, "Good morning Mrs. Schmidt."

Mrs. Schmidt gave him a wide smile that almost enveloped her whole face in wrinkles. "Good morning Bruno. So, you remembered my name!"

"Course I did," said Bruno. "You're a somebody!"

Again, came the squeaky cackle, but this time it lasted a lot longer.

"Hah!" she chuckled. "You learn quick. You'll go a long way!" Bruno waved a hand as if to brush away her words, but he heard them, and they stayed with him. He was a quick learner. You'll go a long way. Mrs. Schmidt had said so. Bruno grinned to himself.

"She needs new bloody glasses as well!" he muttered.

When he got to Mrs. Dwyer's place, she was not on the verandah, but she came out just as he reached the front step. "Oh, good morning Bruno." Instead of waving to Mrs. Schmidt, she turned aside and passed a hand over her forehead, probably a pre-arranged signal, because Mrs. Schmidt came down her steps and started up the street. Bruno looked at Mrs. Dwyer and noticed black circles under her eyes. He knew what that meant. It used to happen to his mum.

"You got a migraine?" he said quietly.

Just as quietly, Mrs. Dwyer said, "A doozy."

Mrs. Schmidt was right there, taking her hand and leading her back inside, away from the bright light. Bruno stepped aside as Mrs. Schmidt spoke in her own language. Mrs. Dwyer obviously understood the words but did not speak herself. She just followed Mrs. Schmidt's instructions and tottered back to bed. Mrs. Schmidt closed the blinds and wrung out a facecloth, which she folded and placed on Mrs. Dwyer's forehead.

Bruno began to worry. What if Mrs. Dwyer had a heart attack or something? How was he supposed to know what to do with a sick old lady? He leaned in the front door and in a loud stage whisper, he asked, "Has she got any painkillers? Panamax, Neurofen, Lyrica, Rafen, any of those?"

Mrs. Dwyer whispered, "Stemetil."

Bruno darted into the kitchen and found them in the smallest cupboard. He handed them to Mrs. Schmidt, who checked the dose and gave the Stemetil to Mrs. Dwyer.

"Is she goin' to be okay?"

Mrs. Schmidt nodded. "She'll be fine, but you can't do noisy work today."

"He can catalog the plants that we'll need for the new garden," came Mrs. Dwyer's weak voice.

"But how will I know?" Bruno almost stuttered.

"Use Desmond's pictures as much as you can. If you can't find them, draw them, and we'll work it out later. There's a spare sketchbook with the others." Mrs. Schmidt shushed her then and signaled for Bruno to leave the doorway.

Bruno went to the deep drawer where Desmond's notes were and fished out the folio and the spare sketchbook. Mrs. Schmidt came out, he said quietly,

"Will I sit here and do the catalog? Should I notify my supervisor?"

Mrs. Schmidt looked him straight in the eye. "You sit here and do what you have to do! Mrs. Dwyer says you're a good young man. We'll see about that. I'll be in the lounge, and if you make so much as a sharp squeak, I'll turn you into Bratwurst!"

Bruno wasn't sure whether to believe her or to laugh at the ridiculous threat, but he saw the worry as she glanced at the closed door of the bedroom and knew it wasn't him that upset her.

"Yer won't even know I'm here," he said and laid out the books, ready to list all the plants he had seen in the garden.

Mrs. Schmidt picked up a magazine and settled herself on a low lounge chair while Bruno sat at the table with the new sketchbook open in front of him. Desmond had made a title page in his book, so Bruno decided to do the same. It would give him a chance to practice with the colored pencils before he tackled the catalog. He was quite good at drawing, although at school, he'd always disrupted the art classes. That was because he never had the right materials, or the coverall for the wet area or a rubber to erase his mistakes. His little tin tray with six cakes of color was always half-worn out, while the other kids squeezed their 12 tubes of poster color all over everything. He had hated those art classes. This was a different kind of drawing, with everything he needed and Desmond's meticulous work as his reference. Bruno soon settled down to do the best possible title page he could. What a sweet cop for Community Service!

He decided to match Desmond's page line for line, but instead of writing.

D. DWYER

GARDEN CATALOG

He wrote,

MRS. DWYER'S NEW GARDEN.

He then copied all Desmond's borders, using the little ruler to check every measurement, selecting the same colors, and being careful to pick the exact shade of yellow and green. He was just finishing the green line when his pencil wobbled, and the line shot off at an angle. "Bugger," he whispered and then checked that he had not disturbed anyone. He grabbed the rubber and tried to ease the line away but smudged it instead. He felt the anger rising and wanted to tear the page out, but he didn't. What he did do - quite accidentally - was knock the pencils, which made a bit of a clatter. He reached down to collect them, and Mrs. Schmidt was at the edge of the table, watching.

"I knocked the pencils," he said, ready to stomp out if she snarled.

Instead, Mrs. Schmidt looked at the page and saw the blemish. "You have been very careful, and that is good work.

But the rubber won't work on the colors, only on soft grey lead - number two or four."

Bruno hadn't even noticed the extra black leads had numbers on them. "I will show you how to fix this mistake," she said, pointing at the veering line. Bruno shrugged. If she made it worse, he would tear the page out.

To his surprise, Mrs. Schmidt took the green pencil and went over his mistake, making it stronger and more defined. He frowned. But then she took a slightly paler green and drew an inverted heart, with his line through the center. He watched, fascinated as a tiny green leaf took shape under her delicate touch.

"Hey, that's cool!" he said, then lowered his voice again. "Did you used ta' be an artist or something?"

Mrs. Schmidt looked down her nose at him. "Not used to. I *am* an artist."

"Yeh, but you're retired now, right?" Bruno wasn't sure if she was having him on.

"An artist does not retire. An artist dies an artist. "She spoke like a preacher. "Art is life. Life without art is death."

"Okay. I just asked," Bruno muttered. "I ain't never met no artists before."

Mrs. Schmidt looked at him, again with that direct stare. "You would have seen their works at school? Bruegel, Van

Eyck, Van Gogh, Rubens, Rembrandt?" Bruno looked blank. She tried more modern names. "Cézanne, Picasso? Andy Warhol?"

Bruno shook his head.

"I...er didn't do art history or any of the fancy subjects. Just readin' and English and math catch-up classes."

"That is not learning!" Mrs. Schmidt caught herself before her voice rose. "They are only the tools for learning. Of course, you must have them, but they are so you can find out about learning!"

"Learning what?" asked Bruno, a bit confused now.

"About life!" she said. "The world! Everything!" "Oh," said Bruno, "You mean like geography and science?" In response, Mrs. Schmidt went back to her chair and came back with the magazine. It was a National Geographic.

She pointed to the little map that was their logo. "This is geography," she said, pointing rapidly to parts of the globe with a pencil. Here is Australia. There is India. That is China. Up here, Russia, in here, Germany, there, America. Geography only teaches you where it is, and what is there."

She opened the magazine and flipped the pages until she came to a line map of Indonesia. There was one brown spot on one of the islands. "See? They start their story with geography, but what you learn is inside the story."

She flipped past the introduction before Bruno could even read the first paragraph. She stopped at the photograph of two young boys standing in the river, up to their waists in the swirling waters, hauling a boat laden with strange vegetables, tying it up to the long poles that supported a house right over the river. The picture was titled 'The Greengrocer's Market Boat'.

"You have seen the geography. You know where this is in the world. But what you should learn is about life in that part of the world. What do you learn from the picture?"

"They're helping their dad take the vegetables to market," Bruno said. *"Hell, he wasn't stupid"*. Mrs. Schmidt shook her head.

"There is no dad. They are the greengrocers, and the boat is their market. They float it along to all the houses along the river delta, and trade with the people who live there."

"Oh? Do they make much money?"

"No money. They don't sell; they trade. Our vegetables for your fish. Our fruit for your chicken."

Bruno looked at their skinny frames. "They don't look like they get much to eat except their vegetables."

Mrs. Schmidt flipped over a few more pages, where a photograph showed the boys standing proudly with their mother and six siblings. "They work to feed their family,"

Mrs. Schmidt said quietly.

Bruno's eyebrows shot up as he counted the heads. "Geez! No wonder they're all skinny!"

Mrs. Schmidt closed the magazine. "Today, you have learned the difference between geography and life," she said, "and even though you have not read their whole story, you will never again mistake one for the other."

Bruno looked at her for a long time, letting her words soak in. Then a slight sound from the bedroom sent Mrs. Schmidt hurrying to tend to Mrs. Dwyer. Bruno returned to his front page and looked thoughtfully at the leaf Mrs. Schmidt had drawn. He copied the drawing and colored in a very similar leaf at the top of the same line as carefully as he could. Then he did the same to all the other lines. Mrs. Schmidt had not offered him any morning tea, so he was quite surprised when she came back into the kitchen and said, "You had better go and have your lunch, Bruno. I will see to Mrs. Dwyer. She said that you could take the books home with you tonight if you need to study the flowers and their names and details. She knows you will look after them carefully."

The supervisor, Steve, came back with Bruno after lunch to check that Mrs. Dwyer was not seriously ill and, standing outside the porch, Mrs. Schmidt explained what the situation was. Steve frowned. "But are you okay about Bruno being here when he can't do the noisy physical work today?"

Mrs. Schmidt turned her disconcerting gaze on the supervisor. "You think Bruno will make me afraid because he is on orders?"

Bruno was interested in this situation.

"Well… er, no, we do vet the boys before we…"

"Mr. Supervisor," the old lady interrupted, "In my country, every boy from the age of seven to 15 was on orders. They cleaned the barns, milked the cows, washed down the abattoirs, swilled the pigs, slopped the privies."

Steve looked flustered, but Mrs. Schmidt continued, "And for what crime? Because they were Jewish!" Steve looked embarrassed.

"Of course, there have been some regimes…" he started, but Mrs. Schmidt had not finished.

"Boys who are beaten and cowed into submission are hurt, and they become what society makes them. They steal, lie, destroy because that is what they have been taught to do. I stole! I lied! And I would do it again to survive!!"

"I only meant to reassure you…" Steve started again. "The boy…"

"The boy has a name," Mrs. Schmidt said more quietly. "Bruno and I, we understand one another." Steve looked at Bruno, who put on an air of complete innocence. "There will not be any trouble," said Mrs. Schmidt firmly. And both Steve and Bruno knew that there had better not be!

Bruno went into the garden and picked a few flowers he did not know. Then he settled down at the kitchen table to find them in Desmond's sketchbook. As Desmond had done, he kept to the alphabetical order, writing the common name and the botanical name but omitting the drawings. That way he could get on with the list more quickly.

After some time, Mrs. Schmidt came to him and said, "I have soup at home. I will go and get it for Mrs. Dwyer. She must have fluids. I will be back in a few minutes. If she calls out, come and get me straight away. RUN!"

Bruno looked up and nodded. "I understand. My mum used to get migraines." Mrs. Schmidt nodded.

"I wondered how you knew so many medicines! See, life has already taught you much, Bruno." With that, she left.

As he continued his list, Bruno thought about what life had taught him. He'd learned to duck! He'd learned a whole dictionary of swear-words. He'd learned how to avoid railway ticket inspectors and police who asked awkward questions. He'd learned that he hated bullies who picked on little guys, and he'd learned that people were a weird mix of carelessness and kindness. Even Rod, when he was in his 'Great Guy' character, would sometimes buy Bruno an ice-cream or give him the money to go to a movie. Bruno, even though he loathed the man, would always take it and say thanks. He never threw it back in Rod's face, did he? "Ahh, ye're weak," he told himself, but he wanted those goodies just like any other kid. That was Rod's hold over him.

Bruno's eyes narrowed. That was Rod's hold over his mother too! All she wanted was some of the good things in life, and Rod held them out like bait! "We were both weak, Mum," he whispered. "We shoulda shucked him off!" For the first time probably in his life, Bruno realized that his mum was vulnerable, just like him, putting up with shit to get an ice-cream. "Geez!" he said "The bloody ice-cream wasn't worth it!"

Mrs. Schmidt returned with a big pot of soup and put it on the stove to warm up. "Mrs. Dwyer hasn't moved," he told her.

"Good. Sleep will help her over the worst part."

Bruno looked at her curiously.

"Were you in a concentration camp?" he asked.

"What have you read?" she asked in her turn.

"Nothin' really. One of the teachers read us the diary of Anne Frank. It was mostly about their hiding place, and it sort of ended when they were sent to the concentration camp. She died."

"Millions died," said Mrs. Schmidt, "but many who did not were put into labor camps. They worked as slaves, and they were fed pig swill. And yes, they stole, and they lied because they were starving."

"Just because they were Jews?"

She nodded. "And it still goes on in other countries, maybe not just the Jews. Look at the refugee camps. Look at the way the war battles destroy cities and leave the civilians trapped in the rubble!"

"Get rid of the blokes at the top," Bruno shrugged.

"And replace them with more of the same?"

As he had once before, Bruno felt he was being reprimanded and didn't know why. "Well, geez, don't blame me. I didn't put them there."

Mrs. Schmidt looked sad for a moment. "No, you didn't, Bruno, and no-one will shoot you for going to the polling booth and choosing the person you want to lead you. You are so lucky!"

"I ain't gonna vote for anyone. They're all crooked."

Mrs. Schmidt frowned. "Then, in another year or two, when you have that privilege, you will be to blame. There is an old saying 'bad things happen when good people do nothing.' You still have much to learn about life."

Bruno was defensive, again without knowing why. "I just mind my own business," he said rather pointedly.

Mrs. Schmidt turned away and went to check on Mrs. Dwyer.

CHAPTER EIGHT

That night, Bruno was restless. He had brought home Desmond's sketchbook to study the plants, but he just couldn't settle. He wandered into the lounge where the TV news was on. There were the usual political stories and a road crash that the news teams were hoping might prove to be a murder. There were war stories and refugee stories, and stories of famine in Africa. Then there was a story about a new display at the National Gallery in Victoria, right in Melbourne. No-one paid much attention, but Bruno picked up on the name 'Van Gogh'. Mrs. Schmidt had mentioned him, and it seemed there was going to be an exhibition of his paintings. They showed a couple of images that Bruno had seen on posters in a T-shirt shop.

"Okay," he said to himself, "I know something about Van Gogh." Only he didn't know what made the artist's paintings so good. The news moved to sports fixtures. Most of the guys sat up and watched this part. After that, only those with a reason to be outside paid any attention to the weather.

Tanner looked up and said, "That Vincent Van Gogh must have done somethin' right. Those paintings of his are worth millions!"

Bruno shrugged. "Lucky him; a self-made millionaire!"

Tanner shook his head. "He didn't make the millions. The art dealers do, though."

Bruno frowned and asked, "Didn't he get a share, or royalties or somethin'?"

It was Tanner's turn to shrug. "Nah. Ya know that song 'Vincent?'"

"Yeah," said Bruno.

"That's him. He did all those paintings and then topped himself!"

Bruno was shocked. "But why? I mean, he must have known he was worth something?"

"I don't really know," said Tanner.

That puzzled Bruno for a long time. He went back to his room and looked at Desmond's illustrations. To him, they looked fantastic, considering they were only colored pencil drawings and not oil paintings. He wondered if they were worth much as works of art. He lay there looking at the drawings for so long that he fell asleep with the book on his chest, still fully dressed.

The next morning, after a very hurried clean-up and no shower, he jumped on the Jolly Bus just as it was changing gears. He had the sketchbook with him and hoped Mrs. Dwyer would be okay. But he also wanted to ask Mrs. Schmidt about Vincent Van Gogh. Why would a guy who knew he was a great artist kill himself?

He signed on at the home and then hurried his pace a little. Sure enough, Mrs. Schmidt was standing there, waving at Mrs. Dwyer. He breathed a sigh of relief. His old doddy was gonna be okay! Slowing down, he said, "Morning, Mrs. Schmidt."

There was no cheekiness in it this morning, nor was there from Mrs. Schmidt.

"I wanted to ask you," Bruno began. He hesitated.

"Ask me what?"

"Why did Vincent Van Gogh top himself?"

For a moment, she frowned, then her face cleared, and she said, "Oh, commit suicide?"

"Yeah," said Bruno. "Surely if he knew he was that great, he wouldn't just chuck it away?"

"Vincent was a very troubled man, Bruno, and he didn't think he was a great artist because he was always learning how the old masters did things. Then, when he came to Paris and saw how Cézanne and his friends were experimenting, he fell into deep despair. He also had an unhappy love affair."

Bruno nodded. "Ah, well yeah, that'll do it every time! Thanks."

He continued to Mrs. Dwyer's little villa.

How many unhappy love affairs had his mother had? Four - not counting his father - maybe more? He couldn't remember. Nor did he really want to.

Mrs. Dwyer was sitting down, but she gave him a wave. "Morning, Mrs. Dwyer.

Glad ye're back on yer feet," he said. He smiled to show that he meant it.

"Thank you, Bruno. I'm much better today, but I'll be taking things a bit easy."

"Will the noise worry you if I pull those training wires out today?"

"I don't think so, but if it does, you can continue your catalog."

Bruno looked down for a moment. "I took Des... Mr. Dwyer's sketch pad home, but I didn't do much. I just sorta got wrapped up in looking at the drawings and how real they look. They're very good, aren't they?"

"Yes, they are very accurate, and Desmond was proud of them."

Bruno screwed his face up, the question forming of its own accord.

"Then why isn't Desm... Mr. Dwyer, an artist like Vincent Van Gogh – or Mrs. Schmidt?"

Mrs. Dwyer looked surprised. "Oh, did Mrs. Schmidt show you her work? That's an honor. She rarely lets anyone see what she has done."

Bruno shook his head.

"No, I didn't see any, but she said she was an artist, like Vincent Van Gogh. Why are their paintings art and these ones," he indicated the sketchbook, "aren't?"

"That's quite a question!" said Mrs. Dwyer, eyeing Bruno with some curiosity. "Basically, what Desmond has done is put down what you see and where things change, so he is drawing the shape and the color of the flower. But genuine artists like Vincent Van Gogh and, yes, Mrs. Schmidt, they somehow breathe life into their paintings."

"But some of his looked... crooked, or out of... kilter," Bruno finished.

"Art isn't about being a perfect image," said Mrs. Dwyer. "You can get that from a photograph. No, they draw, or paint, or sculpt things in such a way that the image becomes the painters' experience of their subject partly; how they fit with their ideas about life."

"Like Star Wars?" said Bruno.

Mrs. Dwyer opened her eyes wide with a snapping movement, then had to close them until her head stopped spinning. "I beg your pardon?"

"Yeah, like Star Wars. I saw this doco on how they take what we know is real, like planets and stuff, and then everything else is all made up from what people think will be out there. So that's what they makeup, a whole imaginary life!"

Mrs. Dwyer gave a bit of a shrug. "Er, well, yes, I suppose you could draw that line…"

Bruno grinned. "Do you think Mrs. Schmidt would let me see some of her paintings? If I said please?"

"Why don't we ask her at morning tea time?"

Bruno took this as a hint to get on with his work, so he did just that!

Steve had issued him with pliers and a wire cutter and a couple of screwdrivers to dismantle the wires that had supported all the vines along the fences, so Bruno went to work trying to get the screws out. No matter what he tried the screw simply would not budge. He tried sliding the blade underneath the wire and levering. That worked with a few. Then he just used wire-cutters and simply cut the wires free, leaving the screws in place. Where they had been stapled, it was much easier to remove the staples and drag the wires clear. There were half a dozen wires across each panel of fencing, so he worked until he heard two voices inside the house. He stopped and gave a stretch, flexing the hand he had injured on the jasmine that first day. It was nearly healed now.

"Bruno, Mrs. Schmidt is here. Coffee's on."

He hopped down off the raised garden bed and ducked in to wash his hands. Then, putting on his best face, he smiled at the ladies. "Thanks, Mrs. Dwyer. Hello, again, Mrs. Schmidt."

The two women exchanged half-amused glances, but they responded in like manner. "You're welcome, Bruno."

"Mrs. Dwyer tells me you'd like to see my paintings."

"Yeah…yes, if you wouldn't mind."

"Where has this sudden interest in art come from?"

Mrs. Schmidt was always direct, straight to the point. "

It just happened. You mentioned Vincent Van Gogh, and then I saw on TV that there's an exhibition at the National Gallery of Victoria, and they showed some of his paintings."

Mrs. Dwyer chipped in, "Bruno is wondering why Desmond was not considered an artist like you, and he hoped you might be able to explain the difference."

Bruno reached for his coffee and took a chunk of cake from the plate alongside it. "Mr. Dwyer's pictures look real, and they're… pretty, you know? Some of the paintings last night looked not quite right - to me anyway."

Mrs. Schmidt gave him one of her direct stares. "Art is not always pretty, Bruno. I said yesterday that art was life. Life is not always pretty."

"Tell me about it!" he muttered, then said more clearly, "I understand that. I've seen war photos, and I've...been around..." He didn't want them to ask questions.

Mrs. Schmidt was staring again.

"So, if I were to paint you, for instance..." Bruno flushed, embarrassed, but she continued staring at him. "I could choose to paint you on that first day. Your face would be the same but with a miserable expression. And I would paint you with your shoulders hunched and your feet dragging through the dust on the gritty road."

Bruno frowned, "But the road here is asphalt!"

Mrs. Schmidt shook her head. "I am not painting the geography," she said, "I am painting how you feel!"

It was Mrs. Dwyer's turn to frown. "Geography?"

"Bruno understands." Mrs. Schmidt studied him again. "But today, I would paint you with tools in your hand, and a garden shed, and a wilderness behind you. And your feet would be bare; free amongst the dandelions."

This time Mrs. Dwyer smiled and said, "And your smile would bring joy to everyone who saw you!"

Mrs. Schmidt nodded in agreement. "Bruno's face was meant to shout joy and happiness to the whole world!"

Bruno flushed again; his embarrassment mixed with a good measure of pleasure. He grinned rather self-consciously, he tried to conceal it. Mrs. Schmidt became business-like again. "And you see, neither of my paintings would be geography."

"No," said Bruno. "They would be parts of my life."

"And parts of mine," said Mrs. Schmidt. "I can just remember the feel of bare feet amongst the dandelions. But I will never forget the ache of feet that are forced to walk along rough roads towards a place of danger."

Mrs. Dwyer broke in as she saw the sadness descend on Mrs. Schmidt.

"Well, perhaps you can talk later if Bruno can see some of your works. Right now, your coffee is getting cold, and your beautiful cake is just begging to be eaten."

Bruno was quiet as he finished his coffee, and when he returned to the garden, he stood for a moment, his tools in his hand, positioning them, first this way and then another, imagining how they would look in a painting. As he started work again, he knew that if he were an artist, he would draw himself with the tools, working. He wondered how he would depict the power in the muscles that pulled at the resistant wires.

He looked around the small garden he was dismantling and thought about how he would draw Desmond in his wheelchair, leaning over to plant things less than a meter away, yet so constrained by his body. Suddenly he understood why sometimes, a photograph couldn't say enough. And why he would need to look at paintings differently. "Every single person who came into this garden would have to be painted in a different way!" he exclaimed.

That afternoon, Mrs. Dwyer told him to leave early, so he would have time to stop at Mrs. Schmidt's. "We know you're not supposed to," she said, "but I think this is one of those rules that needs a bit of bending."

So, Bruno cleaned up a little more carefully, then went down to see Mrs. Schmidt. She opened the door immediately.

"Come in. Mrs. Dwyer said you wouldn't be able to stay long."

"We're not supposed to go anywhere except where we're allocated."

"Oh, in case you're going to check the place out to rob later?"

Bruno grinned. "Not your place! You'd turn us into Bratwurst!"

Mrs. Schmidt burst into her crackly cackle. "I told you that you were a quick learner." And she led him into her living area.

Although the two villa units were mirror images of each other, the two ladies couldn't have been more different. Where Mrs. Dwyer had had a bit of stuff lying around, but all sort of lived-in and cozy, Mrs. Schmidt's living area was as plain and utilitarian as it could be. The benches were bare of any knick-knacks. The furniture was small, sparse, and looked as though nobody sat there much. "Out the back," she said, and he obediently went through to the back garden. Except that there wasn't one.

"GEEZ!"

In fact, the garden area had been roofed over with some of those see-through roof panels so that it was like an extra room. In this part was the most amazing clutter Bruno had ever seen. There were three easels of different sizes, a shelf on the side fence that supported drying canvas and held big tubes of paint and jars full of brushes of every length and thickness. There were old sketchbooks, with newer ones on top of them, lying in a shallow plastic bin – the kind that goes under a bed. This garden room led into the carport space, which had also been enclosed, floored, and lined, so it was an extra room. "This is my gallery," said Mrs. Schmidt, watching to see the effect on Bruno.

Bruno was flabbergasted! The walls were covered, literally from the floor up, with paintings of every size and color that he could think of. But if he was expecting flowers and wilderness scenes, then Bruno was shocked by the images. They were of soldiers, and the Nazi swastika was evident in most of them.

They were in greys, rust colors, and dull greens, and exuded a sense of hopeless despair. And they were 'out of kilter' too. One was of a padlock as big as a truck wheel, and below it all these clutching hands were trying to reach the key and turn it. They were grey claws, and the fingers were skeletal. Many were bleeding, and all the fingernails were blackened and torn. High up in the corner was a stone building with a tall chimney that belched black clouds of stinking smoke. Fleetingly, Bruno wondered how a painting could tell him the smoke stank. "That is called 'Before and After,'" said Mrs. Schmidt, "Before," she pointed to the desperate hand. "After," she said, pointing to the black smoke's fat, heavy whorls of cloud.

"Geez!" came Bruno's voice in a strangled whisper. "It's a gas chamber!"

"No." Mrs. Schmidt's voice was hard-edged. "It's the incinerator. That comes after the gas chamber." She turned to another painting. "This," she said in a somber tone, "this is the gas chamber." This time, all the breath left Bruno's body. It was a cell, only bigger. He could already feel the claustrophobia. But this cell was not for one or two. There must have been 30 people crammed into it, men, women, children, all piteously malnourished and clambering to escape. Some were already dead, held up only by the mass of anguished humanity crammed in beside them. Kids were sliding down the adults' legs, being churned together on the floor.

"Oh, Jeesus!" Bruno gasped. At last, his stomach was heaving. Mrs. Schmidt turned him around and shoved him gently outside. He stood there for a minute, gasping.

"Come in here," Mrs. Schmidt ordered, and he followed like an automaton.

Back in the house, he sat down, and she poured him a small, clear drink.

"It's vodka," she said.

Bruno had often had alcohol in his teenage years, mostly beer or 'plonk', but the vodka ran down his throat like water. Then it burst inside him with the heat of a furnace. His stomach stopped heaving, and his swimming senses cleared.

"When I came to Australia," she told him, "I was in trauma, you know? They sent me to a mental hospital. The doctor told me I had to get all these bad memories out of my mind, or they would destroy me. He suggested I write, but I did not know the English words for such horror. So, they sent me to art classes. There I learned the secrets of lines and shapes and how to paint muscles in light and shade." She looked at him, direct and clear, not excusing, not embellishing, just the truth. Bruno nodded without speaking.

"These were the tools I needed!" she said. "I already had the images, images I had to get out of me." There were shadows in her eyes now, and Bruno knew she was not even seeing him. "It took years and years of therapy," she whispered. "So many faces I should have remembered. So many names I should never forget." She poured herself a shot of vodka and drained it quickly. Then her voice became more normal.

"I have shown you two paintings, Bruno, and I shall not show you anymore. Because in those two you have learned about art and artists. When you see art from the soul, you will know."

"How can you bear to keep them, to ever look at them?" he asked, his voice quite gruff with emotion.

"I don't look at them - except for very special people. But I keep them so that long after I am dead, people will never forget the Holocaust!"

Bruno stood up and took hold of her hand for a moment. "I won't never forget Mrs. Schmidt, never!" Then, full of unfamiliar emotions, he fled out the door and onto the Jolly Bus. It seemed almost disrespectful to be on the stupid bus with the cartoons on its side panels. Bruno couldn't wait to get home and into the privacy of his own space.

He looked around his little room in this shared house for people who didn't belong anywhere. He didn't want to leave it, not even to go down for something to eat. Some kind of weariness sapped his energy, and he fell asleep. He wasn't sure if he was dreaming or just waking, but his room seemed different. Superimposed on its walls, he saw the padlocked cell door of the gas chamber; the emaciated, living yet dead bodies of the people in Mrs. Schmidt's painting; still standing, still struggling for life, even as they were already breathing in the fumes that would kill them.

"Oh, Jesus Christ," he said to himself. "I don't ever want to get stuck in a cell like that."

Bruno made a tentative start at a conversation with Zarb a day or so later.

"Ya know this stuff about a chance to go back to school?"

Zarb's eyes looked sad. Bruno was going to back out.

"Yeah. What's the problem? Having second thoughts?"

"Oh no…It's just that…" he tried to get the words right. "Well, I was pretty smart-arse about treating it like two years in jail." He took a breath and said, "The truth is…I really don't want to go to jail." There was such an intensity in his voice that Zarb turned to examine him.

"What's the matter, Bruno, has somebody been making threats?"

"No," said Bruno, "but I've become sort of interested in art, and I saw a painting of the gas chambers at a concentration camp. It gave me the creeps!"

"Our prisons are hardly like that," Zarb reassured him.

"I know, but the idea is stuck in my mind, and I can't get it out."

"Well, these days, it's not being in their cells that the prisoners feel scared of!"

Zarb was talking of his own experience. Bruno just knew it. "It's bein' out in the yard, or the meal hall, or in the ablutions block. If they're gonna get at ya, that's where they'll do it. They can't touch you once you're safely locked inside your cell. Does that help?"

"Er, yeah," said Bruno doubtfully.

"If I can keep one kid like you out of there, then I'm doin' a good job!" said Zarb. Bruno nodded. Only now he had something else to worry about if he went to jail!

"Anyway, you'll be finished with us soon, and if you do go back to school, you'll make a good fist of it. You're a quick learner."

Bruno looked up in surprise. "How do you know?"

"Why, we've had nothing but good reports about you from everyone at Seven Plains; the lady in the office right down to the maintenance man. They all reckon you're a good lad, and a good worker, with a generous heart, puttin' up with the old busy-body ladies."

"Who? Mrs. Dwyer and Mrs. Schmidt? They're my friends!"

This time the look on Zarb's face was stunned surprise! Bruno the loner? Making friends with a couple of old biddies on his community assignment?

"Well," he smiled, "wonders will never cease!"

CHAPTER NINE

Tanner was watching Bruno that evening as he toyed with his meal once again.

"You been off yer feed a couple of days now. Anything wrong?"

A month ago, Bruno would have snarled, *"Mind yer business."*

Now he looked across at Tanner and said, "Just got a bit on my mind. Y'know, life and stuff."

"Like, tryin' to work out what you're gonna choose to study?"

Bruno looked up, surprised. "No. They'll just put me in to catch-up classes for readin', English and math."

"No, they won't. They go with where you're at with them subjects - those subjects. But you get to choose the others. I'm choosing science and technology; computers an' that."

"What else is there to choose from?"

"There's a list on the notice board. C'mon. I'll show you."

Bruno couldn't believe he hadn't seen the list before. It was as big as a newspaper, and there were dozens of things to choose.

His eyes quickly went to 'W' for welding, but that said 'see metalwork'.

So, he looked up metalwork and found it included welding and metal fabrication, panel beating, technical drawing, and something called 'An introduction to Mechanical Engineering'.

Tanner watched Bruno's finger following the line. "That's a good choice. Plenty of decent jobs among that lot."

"Better than goin' to jail!" Bruno said. He tried to make it nonchalant, but it didn't come off.

Tanner looked at him quickly.

"You been there too," he said as if it were fact.

Bruno didn't deny it, even though he hadn't actually been in any cell except an overnight lock up in the suburbs.

Tanner gave a shiver. "I was there two weeks before they commuted my sentence on appeal. That was enough. Even the funny farm was better than jail. They tell you they'll protect you from all the others. Ergh! Who's gonna protect you from them?"

Bruno was stunned. "They sent you to a mental hospital?" he almost whispered, "But you look so... normal!" Tanner shrugged.

"Normal guys don't go around getting' busted for a major crime." Tanner crossed his eyes and stuck out his tongue in a fair imitation of a gargoyle.

"No shit!" said Bruno.

"Well, it wasn't all my fault," Tanner said somewhat defensively, "Mum would always burn all the bills that came in the envelopes with the little windows. Anyway, when this one comes, I thought I'd save her the trouble and put it in the fire," he paused. "The problem was, it was a court order to say she'd be fined 1,000 dollars if she ignored it. Of course, she never read it, so she ignored it."

"Oops!" Bruno could think of nothing else to say.

"Yeah, well, the bloke she was livin' with turned real nasty, and he was belting me around. He'd started doin' that when I was 10. Anyway, when Mum stood up for me, he belted her too." Bruno reckoned he knew what was coming next, and his heart went out to the 10-year-old Tanner. "So, I grabbed his bookie's bag and chucked all his betting slips into the fire as well; tote notes, cash, debtor's markers, the lot! The updraft blew burning paper everywhere and set the whole house on fire!"

"No shit!" said Bruno, but this time his voice was open admiration.

"Shit ain't the half of it!" said Tanner ruefully. "He couldn't pay out his bets, see, and he went belly up…bankrupt! The bastard told Mum I had to be put away, and it was him or me. When she said it was me, he belted her across the mouth and knocked some of her teeth out. She was too scared to say anything after that." Bruno was surprised that there was no blame in Tanner's voice. Tanner noticed his look and said, "I knew she didn't have any choice. She's never had a choice, not in her whole life."

Somewhere in Bruno's brain, a trip hammer was pinging, but he couldn't quite concentrate on it right now. But another thought, different now, suddenly came clear to him with new sympathy for his mother. "Neither did mine, really. I don't think she ever had a decent chance."

Tanner looked at the list on the wall again, and said, "There are some electives you can do if you're not into sport."

"I like sport," said Bruno, "but I always do my block and get sent off."

"Then do a solitary sport, instead of a team sport," said Tanner. "I'm gonna do weightlifting."

Bruno just stopped himself from laughing. Tanner was such a stringy sort of build. It was a preposterous choice. Still, the idea of a solitary sport appealed to him. "I might do swimming." He jabbed his finger at the list and then noticed art – history, and appreciation. "And I'll do that too!" he announced.

Tanner looked up, surprised. "Most of the guys are taking the bare minimum of four subjects."

Bruno shrugged. "Maybe I got more to make up for than they have!"

Tanner looked at the list again. "I might do that one too!" he said, "I don't know hardly anything about art. Maybe I can become a rich art dealer."

"Art isn't about the money," Bruno said airily, "It's about life!" Suddenly hungry, he went to raid the fridge for something to eat.

On Monday, Bruno finally got around to telling Mrs. Dwyer that he had taken up the offer of returning to school. She was delighted with his decision but puzzled that he wasn't going to look for work. "But how will you live? And I thought you'd be free of corrections after you finished here!" she said.

"Yeah, but it's an offer too good to refuse!! And we get an allowance to pay rent and food and all that." Bruno grinned. "Anyway, even if life is really shitty, you can get away and start again. Mrs. Schmidt did!"

Mrs. Dwyer nodded without speaking. Bruno hesitated for a minute and then said, "We're not supposed to be stickybeaks either, but do you know how she escaped?"

Mrs. Dwyer hesitated only for a moment and then said, "It was near the end of the war. The allies were gaining ground, and the Germans had to retreat. They dug these huge mass graves and tried to bury the evidence. They thought the little girl was dead, you see, so they threw her out of the truck into the pit grave. But they hadn't finished filling it in when the order came to withdraw." Bruno was horrified at the image forming in his mind. "One of the locals heard muffled crying." Bruno remembered the children who sank to the floor of the gas chamber. He felt his eyes sting. "There were three still alive, but the other two died from dirt in their lungs. They pulled the surviving girl out and cared for her. They would have been shot if they'd been caught, but the war ended not long after that, and all the children were taken away. She - our Mrs. Schmidt, - was sent to a displaced persons' orphanage out here in Australia. It took her nearly 10 years in a psychiatric hospital for her to recover." Bruno nodded, quite unable to speak. "She won't show me her paintings, you know," she said, "only her recent landscapes or urban scenes." She tapped him on the forearm. "You are a very privileged young man!"

"I'm really glad I'm me and not them!" Bruno said fervently.

Mrs. Dwyer decided he needed some physical distraction. "The maintenance man has cleared the bed across the front for you," she said. "You can start removing the retaining wall today." Bruno was happy to oblige. He worked with a will, forcing his mind and his muscles to the task. He tried not to think about all the events of the past few days.

He shipped out soil with the wheelbarrow all that week, then went back and removed another layer of the bluestone pitchers. His idea was to not just pile them up, but to rebuild them as a wall on the other side of the roadway. They were not so high, but the wall was longer, and it gave a sort of finish to the end of the estate.

One morning Mrs. Schmidt wasn't on the porch. She didn't come over for morning tea, and she wasn't on the porch the next morning either. "D'yer think she's okay?" he asked Mrs. Dwyer when he arrived.

"Oh yes, she's fine. She's gone to Melbourne to see the Van Gogh exhibition you told her about. She's staying a few days with friends."

Bruno breathed a sigh of relief. "I'm glad," he said, "She's ..." Nice didn't seem right somehow. Mrs. Dwyer was nice. Mrs. Schmidt was "interesting."

"Mrs. Schmidt is a person!" laughed Mrs Dwyer, imitating the German accent.

"I wish I coulda gone with her to the exhibition!" he said.

There was a tinge of hunger in his voice that made Mrs. Dwyer look up. "Well, it's on for a few weeks. You could still go." But she knew that he would not go on his own.

That afternoon while Bruno was washing up, she slipped out to the office and had a word to Steve. Then she went back to her unit with a self-satisfied smile on her face.

On Friday night, when the boys were hanging around waiting for the footy to start on the telly, Steve came over to Bruno and Tanner, who seemed to sit together these days.

"I've been given a couple of tickets for the Van Gogh exhibition. Would you like to go, Bruno?"

Bruno shot out of his seat. "Would I! Are you going?"

"No," said Steve, and Bruno's face fell.

"What about you, Tanner? I see you're on the list for art appreciation."

"Sure!" said Tanner. "I'd love to!" Bruno's face lit up again.

"Well, I've printed out the train timetable, and I have the directions from Southern Cross," said Steve, producing the papers, along with the printouts of their entry tickets.

Bruno reached for the tickets, but Steve flipped them just out of reach. "You'll be trustees," he warned. "Very best behavior, no cheek to the attendants or any other bullshit?"

"My oath!" said Tanner.

"Or I'll be a Mrs. Schmidt's Bratwurst!" laughed Bruno! That threw Steve for a moment, but he handed over the paperwork.

The next day the boys were up and dressed early. They were clean, and their jeans and shirts were ironed. Their hoodies, however, looked a trifle the worse for wear. They were surprised then when the housekeeper called them over and said, "I was at the op-shop yesterday, and I picked up these. They'll keep you warmer in this wind." And she handed them each a near-new hoody. The boys were quick to swap their old ones, and the housekeeper said she would put them in with the laundry. So it was that two quite respectable-looking young men went off to catch the train to the city.

If Mrs. Schmidt had been there to paint them, she would have seen two young men with a spring in their step, their hoods flung back, and their smiling faces open to the sky. There was none of the truculence that had shrouded Bruno's face a few short weeks ago and none of the fear of sudden movement that had kept Tanner ever-watchful around strangers.

Together they boarded the train with all the confidence of genuine ticket holders, and for once looked at everything except their feet. They didn't talk a lot because it was a new experience for both of them to feel that they had the right to be there. And so, they had. Nobody on the train thought otherwise. Bruno particularly noticed the difference from his last train ride, when he'd been shoved into the guard van - 'made an example of'.

When they got out at Southern Cross, Tanner said, "Zarb gave me 10 dollars to get something to eat."

Bruno laughed and said, "Steve gave me 20 for the two of us."

So, they grabbed some hot chicken and chips and then walked over to the tram stop. Neither of the boys had spent much time in the city proper. It was a bit of a shock to find so many homeless people spreading a tarp out to claim a bit of footpath that they could call home. An old bloke came forward and said, "Spare us 10 dollars, mate? I ain't eaten for two days."

Tanner stopped eating the chicken and chips he had just bought and handed it over saying, "Here you are old-timer. You can have this. It's still hot."

"I can get a feed cheap," the man said shaking his head. "Just give me the 10 dollars."

"I haven't got 10 dollars," said Tanner, holding out the parcel again. The man swore and swept it out of his hand. "Fuck!" Tanner exploded. "That's the last good turn I do for anyone."

A youngster a few years younger than themselves streaked across the pavement and grabbed the packet of chicken and chips off the footpath.

"You're doin' me a favor, mate. I really haven't eaten since yesterday morning!"

He wolfed down the food with relish. Bruno had bought a Coke, and he handed that over. The boy grabbed it. He nodded towards the older man, who was ambling away. "He's on the sauce. All he wants is money for grog."

"Where do you sleep?" asked Bruno. "Ya got a community aid service?"

The boy laughed. "You're kiddin', right? There's the Gill or Ozanam House. First in gets the bed."

"What about the Salvos?" asked Tanner.

"Yeh, they help where they can. Them and St. Vinnies run soup kitchens, but most of us just muck out right here on the street."

"The Brotherhood of St. Lawrence used ter be pretty good," said Bruno.

"Well, good luck mate," said Tanner.

"Yeah. Thanks for the food," replied the youngster as they went on their way.

"Funny," said Bruno, "you always think that you're the only one with troubles."

"Yeah," said Tanner. "The only one!"

They caught their tram up Collins Street instead of Flinders Street because that gave them a chance to look around the city itself. The map said if they got out near the State Library, they could just walk down Swanston Street and over the bridge. From the library, the bridge looked a bit of a way, and the National Gallery looked even further.

"Our train tickets give us free travel for an hour," Tanner said. "Let's ride down and walk back."

So, they hopped on a tram and headed straight for the National Gallery of Victoria.

It was a massive building of grey stone, with a moat out the front. A concert hall stood next door, underneath a tall white cone construction that 'Melbournites' called 'The Witch's Hat.' Both boys stood for a while, just looking at the entrance. The doors were at either end of a large glass arc, with trickles of water constantly flowing down its surface. "It's reticulated from the moat," Tanner said.

"Re-what?"

"Reticulated. The water is sucked up and sprayed out over and over again."

"Mmm," said Bruno. "Remind me to ask for you as a tutor for my English class!"

"One thing," grinned Tanner, "ya'd never have to clean the windows!"

There was already a special queue for the Van Gogh exhibition. The boys waited more or less patiently until their group was allowed through. A tour guide was waiting for them, and the two got upfront so they'd be able to see without too many people in front of them. Bruno wanted to hear what the guide would say. It was Tanner who was the one who was all agog. "Did you hear what the guide said? This Van Gogh guy couldn't afford to buy paints. He had to make his own colors and everything! You'd need to be an analytical chemist to do that now! And what if he used mercury or something? He'd die if the stuff got on his skin!"

Bruno just nodded. He was studying the pictures, looking for the keys that made Vincent such an artist. He saw the lines and the patient cross-hatchings. He saw the first, or second or third treatment of some subjects. He saw the lines of paint, so thickly textured and so lavishly applied, and thought, "For a man who couldn't afford paint, he sure used a lot of it!" But as he went from image to image, the thought that kept returning was the sheer frustration of the man who was trying to get it right. He stopped noticing that the wicker chair was a bit off in the corners. Instead, he noticed the sag of the wicker where the odd thread had slipped in its groove, and the soft sagginess of the seat. *"Vincent has sat in that chair a lot,"* he said to himself. *"He's painted in the dents from his bum!"*

When they stood and looked at the image that inspired 'Vincent', the song 'Starry Starry Night,' Tanner frowned and said, "There's no constellation in the sky that looks anything like that!"

And Bruno said, "He's not painting geography. It's more about Star Wars."

"You're nuts," Tanner said, "Star Wars isn't that old!"

"I don't mean the movie exactly," said Bruno, still staring, "I mean he's dreaming of what he might find if he could just reach out and touch them."

"How do you know?" demanded Tanner.

"Because I can feel him reaching out, trying to catch the stars on the end of his brush!" said Bruno.

At this point, the guide smiled, turned around to his group, and said, "There you have it, ladies and gentlemen. Our young art student has hit the nail on the head!" Then to Bruno, he said, "Well done, young man. You're a credit to your college!" Bruno nearly fell over, and Tanner was choking back his laughter so much he started to sputter. The tour guide frowned at him, and he quickly got himself under control. The tour continued without further incident.

Once they were back in the entrance foyer, they looked at all the signs to the various galleries, and Bruno said to Tanner, "D'ya wanna look at some of the others as well, so that we have some comparison?"

Tanner gave an off-hand nod, so they went off to look at a few of the other collections. They found the one called 'The Heidelberg School'. There were no paintings of any schools, but a lot of sunlit bushland and gum trees, with the odd farm in a few of them. Bruno went up to an attendant and said, "Are the farmhouses the old Heidelberg schools?"

The attendant looked at him for a minute before clearing her throat and said, "No. The Heidelberg School is the group of artists." Bruno felt his face burn. "They used to go out and paint country scenes around Heidelberg before it was a suburb. A 'school' is a certain type of art, like…er, the Impressionists, for instance."

"Impressionists?" asked Tanner.

"Yes, like Cézanne or…"

"Cézanne," said Bruno, grabbing at a name he'd heard. "Do you have any of his paintings here?"

"Well, as a matter of fact, we do. A philanthropist has a Cézanne on loan to the Gallery for a short while. It's upstairs to the right of the Van Gogh collection."

Bruno thanked her and they went up the escalator once more to find the Cézanne. "I've seen copies of that before," said Tanner, looking at the little boats sailing across the sheltered bay. "It's very splotchy up close."

"Yes, I can see that," said Bruno, squinting his eyes and looking at the picture.

"What are you doing?"

"Mrs…This lady told me that when Van Gogh got to Paris, he saw how Cézanne was doing it, and he had to go home and start to learn painting all over again."

"So?"

"I'm just trying to see it the way Vincent would have seen it."

"Then you'd see blobs instead of lines," said Tanner. "The tour guide said Van Gogh started as an engraver. Everything he drew had lines all over it, lines, like the engraving pen for our bike frames."

In the blobs, Bruno saw what Vincent would have seen, the lack of precision, the absence of fine detail. Yet the blobs were clearly boats, and the water was clearly a sheltered bay.

"You're right, Tanner," he said. Tanner looked puzzled.

"Am I?"

And so, their day sped by until they couldn't look at one more painting for fear their eyes would shut down of their own accord.

When they got outside, the thought of walking back to Southern Cross made them both shake their heads. They caught the tram back to Collins Street and then another tram back to Southern Cross. They checked the timetable and just had time to catch the Seven Plains train that would take them home.

"Well!" said Tanner. "I reckon that was the weirdest day I ever spent without getting into trouble. But it was good." Bruno nodded, but he was very quiet all the way home.

CHAPTER TEN

The community project at Seven Plains would soon be finished, and Bruno had picked up the habit of taking Desmond's books home with him every night to finish the catalog of plants for Mrs. Dwyer's new garden. He didn't know that she had paid for him to go to the exhibition, and he didn't tell her he'd been. There was something about it he wanted to keep private just yet. The experience had moved him in some way, but he wasn't quite sure how.

Mrs. Dwyer was rather disappointed. She had expected him to arrive on Monday morning, bubbling over about the weekend. When he didn't, she felt she could hardly bring it up. So, she decided the whole thing must have been a disappointment to him. She mentioned it to Mrs. Schmidt, who just said it was best to let the boy be for the moment. "He is still digesting it." Then she cackled. "That boy has a quick mind, but it's all over the place. He's like a kid in life's lolly shop; he doesn't know how to take it all in." Mrs. Dwyer agreed to let him be. Any disappointment she felt seemed trivial compared with the disappointments that were strewn through other people's lives.

So, the week passed quickly, with Bruno suddenly anxious to make his work the best he could make it. And it wasn't just for the good report anymore. He wanted to leave Mrs. Dwyer a place where she could manage the garden by herself. After some discussion with the maintenance man, they agreed that they should leave two rows of the bluestone pitchers in place so that Mrs. Dwyer would not have to bend over to manage her plants. Bruno had dug in bags of compost and potting mix and a bit of river sand all mixed in together. He'd turned over every meter of the soil until the earth felt like damp sawdust and crumbled in his fingers.

Bruno had also taken all the dirt he'd removed from her garden and packed it along the low wall he had made at the end of the road. Here he carefully transplanted the old snapdragons that were still blooming defiantly and put in some of the smaller plants that the maintenance man had told him were okay to transplant, like the smaller rosemary and a miniature agapanthus. "You can't kill them with a stick!" the maintenance man had said. The people who lived in the last two houses were quite pleased to have the garden wall and would smile at Bruno as he delivered his next wheelbarrow load.

"Well, it looks better than a rubbish heap!" was all he said. He smiled a lot more these days.

For the last two days of Bruno's community order, he and Mrs. Dwyer chose the plants to go in the new garden and started replanting. They had plenty of cuttings to choose from, so there was really no need to buy new ones. But on the last day, Bruno arrived with a Magna-tray of 15 new plants.

As soon as he arrived, he thrust them up at Mrs. Dwyer. "These are for you," he said with a bit of a growl. "Going away present."

Mrs. Dwyer was surprised - and delighted. "Oh! Snapdragons! That's a brilliant touch, Bruno. I wonder how long these will keep going?"

"Well, ya oughta get three years at least," he said.

"We'll have to add them to our new garden book."

"I added 'em in last night," he said. "The book's finished."

He unslung a bag from his shoulder, and Mrs. Dwyer said, "Well, before you get mud on you, bring it in and let's have a look."

Bruno went into the kitchen with her, and they put the books on the table. Then Mrs. Dwyer opened Bruno's catalog. When she saw the title page, she smiled and said, "You've made the two books a matched set! That's nearly the same as Desmond's title page. I love the little leaves you added."

"Mrs. Schmidt did the first one. I just copied hers."

Mrs. Dwyer turned over the next page and gave a sort of gasp. Then, without speaking, she continued to turn the pages. Bruno was getting the fidgets. "You don't like it," he said, as his spirit drooped.

"Bruno, I love it! I can't believe you were capable of such work! This catalog is truly amazing!"

Bruno's smile came back as if she had turned on a light. In the catalog he had drawn all the plants and flowers. They were not specimens like Desmond's, nor were they as expertly executed. But they were the flowers from her garden, no-one else's; plants he had grasped and knew the feel of. The jasmine had a line of red along its wiry vine, where he had cut his hand. Above the rosemary leaning over the bluestone, he'd drawn a tiny bee, hanging like a miniature helicopter coming into land. The yellow climbing roses were scrambling up the new wire beside the rusted screws. Tall stalks of irises stuck their leaves up like kids in a classroom. Then, in the dirt, alongside a tangle of stringy vine roots, he had drawn the dark impression of his boot print.

"Oh, we have to show this to Mrs. Schmidt!" she said. "Quick, Bruno. Your legs are younger than mine. Go and get her. Don't say anything about the book. Just say, can she come straight away. You better tell her there's nothing wrong."

With his heart turning over like a Kawasaki, Bruno ran down the road to Mrs. Schmidt's unit. As soon as he knocked, she opened the door and straight away said, "Mrs. Dwyer? Another migraine?"

"No, no, she said to tell you there's nothing wrong, but can you come straight away?"

Mrs. Schmidt didn't even wait to lock her door but hurried after Bruno to her friend's house. When she saw Mrs. Dwyer sitting calmly at the table, she said, "So, what are you trying to do, give me a heart attack?"

Mrs. Dwyer smiled and said, "Bruno just nearly gave me one! Come and look at this!" Mrs. Schmidt recognized the sketchbook and opened the front page, nodding at Bruno's added leaves. When she opened the next page, she too was silent, turning the pages one by one very slowly, taking in all the added detail in the pencil sketches.

When she had finished, she looked at Bruno for a long time. Then she went back to the title page. She pointed to a blank space. "An artist signs his work," she said simply.

Bruno beamed. Mrs. Dwyer found him a pen, and he signed his name in the space. "Bruno Capello."

"So, you will continue and become an artist?" asked Mrs. Dwyer.

Bruno shook his head. "No. I thought about it, but I went to see Vincent Van Gogh's paintings and Cézanne, and the artists from the Heidelberg School." The two women looked at each other in surprise.

"No wonder he has indigestion!" said Mrs. Schmidt. Bruno threw her a look that distinctly said, 'She's lost the plot!'

Mrs. Dwyer said, "And you saw something in the paintings that discouraged you?"

"Yeah, sort of," Bruno said. "It's like they were all struggling to get the paintings exact. I got the feeling they would never ever be satisfied or happy with what they did. Desmond wasn't like that. He was really happy with what he did, even though it wasn't 'artist' art."

"This is a great lesson that you have learned, Bruno," said Mrs. Schmidt softly, and her eyes were gleaming. Surely, she wasn't crying over him?

"I still like to look at proper artists' art," he continued, "cos' now I try to work out how they were seeing what I'm looking at. But I don't want to spend my life doing something that will make me miserable. Life does enough of that already."

"So, what will you do when you go back to school?" asked Mrs. Dwyer.

Bruno shrugged. "I've been really happy here because I have changed something good but out of control. Now we've made it even better because it's under control. I might see if I can do horti… gardening."

"Horticulture."

"I'm going to do metal fabrication as well because that's got an introduction to mechanical engineering. Maybe I can do more than I thought I could do."

"Your artistic talent will help you a great deal in both of those subjects," said Mrs. Schmidt. "You must be able to imagine the things you wish to make, and accurate drawing will be a tool to help you make better models."

Bruno smiled, "Yeah, well, first I have to finish making my garden. My hours are up after today."

"Your hours will never be 'up' Bruno," said Mrs. Schmidt. "You will carry these hours with you all your life, and you should be very proud of them!"

"I agree!" said Mrs. Dwyer closing the sketchpad. "But you're right. I need my garden finished before my righthand man leaves the premises!" Bruno went out to plant the snapdragons and finish the garden bed, while Mrs. Dwyer walked to the front porch with Mrs. Schmidt.

Bruno worked through his coffee break, although Mrs. Dwyer brought a mug out for him. He would take a swallow or two but kept working. The 15 new snapdragons were standing along the sunlit streak at the base of the back fence. He could almost see their defiance as they grappled for new footholds in the soil and stretched their pointy little bunches of leaves towards the sun.

The single jasmine was now trained around a single wire that could climb along both walls but not spread their vines everywhere and toss all their perfumed white flowers into next door. One happy wanderer did the same at the other corner. The yellow climbing roses, looking very subdued after a major pruning, were neatly clipped to alternate wires stretched across the back fence. When they bloomed next year, they would be like a golden wall carpet as a background to the other flowers.

Mrs. Dwyer came to help with the small plants along the garden's front edge. The deep blue of lobelia mixed with white and mauve alyssum and tiny violas that Mrs. Dwyer called johnny jump ups. Behind them, a row of sunny-faced pansies shone like small multi-colored plates. They had replanted the daffodil bulbs and the grape hyacinths, ready for the spring.

By late afternoon the garden was complete. Bruno and Mrs. Dwyer regarded it together, each feeling a sense of accomplishment, mixed with sadness that this companionable friendship would end at five o'clock. At last, Bruno gave a sigh and went to wash up. When he came into the kitchen to say goodbye, Mrs. Dwyer was waiting for him. In her hand she had an unsealed envelope.

"It didn't seem right to think that you just 'clocked up your hours' here, when you have done such an excellent job," she said. "I was told on no account to pay you for what you have done because it is you who is paying your debt to society." Bruno nodded. He knew some people did slip a kid five dollars. Instead, Mrs. Dwyer held out the envelope. Bruno pulled out the folded page inside and read,

'To whom it may concern,

I have employed Bruno Capello for some time as a casual garden assistant. During that time, he has been punctual, industrious, and eager to learn. I cannot recommend him too highly for his work ethic and reliability, and I wish him every success in his future life.'

It was signed,

Mrs. B Dwyer, Past President, Save The Children Fund (retired)

Bruno gulped, and his throat refused to work. He was scared that he might burst into tears, so he took out his hanky and blew his nose very hard.

Mrs. Dwyer wasn't even pretending; her eyes were swimming as she took his hand to shake it. "It has been my privilege to meet you, Bruno," she said. "I hope your new life leads you to a happy future."

Bruno couldn't help it. He withdrew his hand and instead reached around Mrs. Dwyer and gave her the biggest hug! "It's been a real pleasure," he croaked, then turned and literally ran out the front door before he started to cry.

Mrs. Schmidt was also on her porch, ready to wave him goodbye. Bruno jumped up the two steps and gave her a bear hug too before he shot off to catch the Jolly Bus and close the door on his brush with the law. The two women just nodded at each other. They both knew that they would miss this young man who had entered their lives so abruptly.

CHAPTER ELEVEN

It was weeks later, almost 11 o'clock on Saturday morning, when Mrs. Dwyer's doorbell rang. Running her fingers through her hair, she opened the door to find Steve, the supervisor standing there. On either side of him were two young men, neatly dressed, wearing almost new hoodies, and sporting two of the widest smiles she had ever seen.

"Good morning Mrs. Dwyer," said Steve cheerily.

"Good morning," she said, somewhat taken aback. "Is anything wrong?"

Steve said, "No, nothing at all. It's just that we don't encourage our boys to become emotionally involved when they're working on community orders, but…"

Mrs. Dwyer interrupted hurriedly, "Oh, but Bruno wasn't to blame. It was I who broke the guidelines and asked him questions about his situation."

"No, no, nothing like that," Steve waved her protest away, "it's just that these two are out of our jurisdiction now. They are free to be friends with whomever they choose - except criminals, of course." Mrs. Dwyer gave a short laugh as if she had just smelt something stale. "But, under the circumstance, I thought the boys would like to say thank you in person for the tickets to the Van Gogh exhibition."

Mrs. Dwyer put up her hand to shush him but was too late. Anyway, it was obvious the boys already knew. So, she just smiled and said, "Won't you come in?" which they did.

Bruno thought the room looked smaller with three big blokes like frogs, ready to jump up and take off. "Would you like tea or coffee?"

"Tea please," said Steve.

"Coffee," said the other two, adding a lame, "please." Mrs. Dwyer put on the kettle and got out four cups.

Steve said, "I don't think you've met Tanner before. He was on a different project."

"Nice to meet you Mr. Tanner," said Mrs. Dwyer from the bench.

"Oh, that's not my surname. It's a nickname because I use to be a runner for a bookmaker."

Steve looked at him, puzzled. "That can't be right. On your papers your mother said it was a childhood nickname."

"I didn't know that!" said Tanner.

"It's an English slang word for sixpence," said Mrs. Dwyer.

Tanner had a funny look on his face. "Somebody used to call me sixpence," he said. "When I was real little. I can't remember who, though. But I remember my mum saying once that for one little sixpence, I sure ate a lot of dollars worth." He looked down at the floor, trying to remember.

Mrs. Dwyer had turned pale and become very still. "Why did they call you little sixpence?"

Her question was very soft, and Bruno caught something in it. He looked up and saw that hungry, searching look on her face. And the trip hammer in his brain suddenly started to clamor.

He looked across at Tanner and said, "I gotta tell her, Tanner. I gotta tell her what you did."

Turning to Mrs. Dwyer, he said, "Tanner burned a house down!"

Tanner, completely stunned by the exposure, said, "Why would she care?"

And turning to Mrs. Dwyer, he said, "They called me sixpence because my name is Zac-"

Bruno and Mrs. Dwyer finished it for him. "Zachary!"

The End.

AUTHOR'S NOTE:

Bruno and Zachary are fictional, but every experience they recount is real to a child somewhere in Victoria. The alternative NSW school is real, and was featured on the ABC, including interviews with students. Mrs. Schmidt was a real person whose name has been changed. As a child, she was rescued from a mass grave during the German retreat. She was still living in 1997, and still bore the numbers that were tattooed on her forearm in the labor camp.

K.V. McLennan